PRINT IN THE SNOW
Anna's Adventure In The Wyssun World

by

E.V. SVETOVA

with illustrations by

MARINA BOTYLEVA

ANANKE PRESS

Print In The Snow: Anna's Adventure In The Wyssun World
Published by Ananke Press Copyright © 2019 by E.V. Svetova

Interior and cover design by Ananke Press
Illustrations by Marina Botyleva

ISBN: 978-0984904044

Ananke Publishing Group LLC, 178 Columbus Avenue, #230137, New York, NY 10023
anankepress.com
info@anankepress.com

First Edition: 2011

Print In The Snow

Anna's Adventure
In The Wyssun World

E.V. Svetova

with illustrations by Marina Botyleva

 ANANKE PRESS

An inside joke shared between two skiing friends twenty years ago has mutated into a monster in its own right. Much love and gratitude to Irina Maslova for all the good times and inspiration.

Chapter I
In which Anna finds herself in a really dark predicament

t's been snowing since morning. All you want to do on a day like this, is stay in bed and watch the snow fall. That is, if you can't go out and ski. One thing you don't want to do, is cut sticky brown tape, rip apart cardboard boxes, and unpack piles of rumpled clothes and stacks of dusty books. Next to packing, unpacking is probably the worst way to spend a snowy day.

The street, the trees, the whole unfamiliar city outside Anna's window looked unclear through the veil of falling snow. Faded like an old photograph. Blurry like she'd been crying all night. She hadn't been. She hadn't cried for over a year. She didn't cry that day, when they pulled her out of Social Studies, took her to the principal's office, and told her about Dad. Even at the funeral, when everybody cried, she didn't. She didn't cry months later, after they had that first huge fight with Mom about the new guy, and after Mom announced they she and the new guy were getting married, and when she was told they were moving to New York. Even when all the girls on the ski team were sniffling, and the bleary-eyed coach was giving a flowery farewell speech about losing his most promising athlete, she didn't shed a tear. It wasn't like she was trying hard to keep cool. Her eyes just felt empty.

Anna sat down on the edge of a box. Something cracked inside, making her jump up; she stumbled over a duffel bag on the floor and crashed head-first into a closet door. This new room of hers was not much bigger than her old room's closet.

And this was considered to be a big apartment. So what if a three bedroom in Manhattan was worth more than their whole house in Michigan? Doing laundry in the common basement was still lame.

She rubbed her bumped forehead, and stared wistfully at the view outside the window. The snowfall had subsided and now only single soft flakes were floating on the air. It was a good weather for skiing.

Anna rolled her eyes, and sighed. No, there would be no skiing. Not today, not tomorrow, not ever. Her new school didn't even have a Nordic team.

Her cross-country racing skis were already lovingly unpacked, and now gleamed against the wall next to the window. Why did she even bother to unpack them? Anna caressed the smooth plastic, feeling the familiar itch: right now, more than anything in the world she wanted to go for a run. Since Dad had been gone, skiing was Anna's secret way of making all the worries disappear – ironic, considering that when he'd been alive, Dad had always been too busy to make it to her big races. He didn't think skiing was a real sport, not like football or softball. They even fought about it. He never got to see how good she was at it, probably even good enough for a college scholarship in a couple of years, at least that's what her coach said. And, unlike some people, her coach never lied.

She grabbed her green ski jacket from the top of the clothes pile, about to hang in the closet.

"Annie, are you done with the textbooks?" Mom called from the corridor. Anna hated when Mom called her that. That name belonged in the old life when Mommy and Daddy and Annie were a happy family. And that life was a lie anyway.

"Almost!" Anna yelled.

"Almost doesn't count!" her mother shot back from the doorway. Her cheeks flushed, a smile of excitement fluttering about her face. It occurred to Anna that her Mom just loved all this: the fuss of moving, the challenge of the new city. The new life.

"Annie, it's been a week since we moved, your new school starts next week, and you haven't even unpacked your books.

Look, you want to be treated like an adult and I trusted you to set up your own room the way you wanted, but you can't live out of the boxes. We've already turned James' office into a storage. What a mess."

Mom surveyed the space, still smiling, like she's seen something funny.

"And why is your skiing gear all over the place? Didn't we agree that it goes into the storage?"

"But what if I want to go for a run?"

"Annie, we've been over this. This is New York City, you don't just go skiing in the park."

"Why not?" Anna didn't like how whiny the sound of her voice came out.

"Because you don't know who you might meet. I'm surprised I have to explain this to you again. James says, it's not okay for a fourteen-year-old girl to go work out in the park alone."

"Of course he would say that, he's a cop, he sees criminals everywhere. It's called paranoid."

"It's not paranoid to be careful with strangers."

"Yeah, like, you were careful marrying the first guy you met on an online dating site," Anna muttered under the breath.

Mom's smile faded.

"It wasn't a dating site, it was a grief support group," she said. "And you know that."

"Whatever."

"Annie, I know you're going through a lot," began Mom, and Anna realized that if she didn't nip this conversation in the bud, Mom would cross the threshold into the room, sit on the bed and try to have one of those talks about feelings. "I always tried to be open with you. I wish you talked to me..."

"There is nothing to talk about," said Anna quickly.

For a moment Mom lingered in the doorway, as if waiting for her to say something, but Anna kept staring out of the window.

"Annie, I can't bring back the life we had," said Mom finally. "James is not your Dad, but he is a good man, a decent man. He is really trying to do right by us. I don't expect you to love him right away, but just try to give him a chance, give this new life a chance…"

With a groan of exasperation, Anna fell backwards on the unmade bed, pulling her ski jacket over her head like a blanket. This talk about being open made her want to throw up.

She may have never had a boyfriend or even kissed a boy, but she wasn't stupid. She had known for two weeks now. Exactly the day before the move, when the house had been packed up and the moving truck already parked in their driveway, Anna was taking the trash out and accidentally tore the trash bag. Well, perhaps it hadn't been entirely an accident, she had been feeling pretty angry about a lot of things, so she may have kicked the bag a little before dumping it into the trash can. That was when she saw that pink and blue box in the bathroom trash, the same stupid generic drug store pregnancy test they were shown in Sex Ed earlier that school year.

So, she saw the box, and it all came together: how Mom asked for extra pickles with her Reuben sandwich at the diner, how James wouldn't let her lift a single box when they packed, and how they both had that happy and guilty look, like they had a secret. Except, Anna knew exactly what it was: Mom was having a baby with her new husband, and she didn't even bother telling her own daughter. All the talk about treating her as an adult was just another lie. Probably, because Anna didn't matter anymore. With the new husband, the new home and the new baby on the way, clearly, there was no place for Anna in this whole arrangement.

"Life is complicated sometimes," continued Mom. "It can seem messy…"

"Well, enjoy your mess and I'll enjoy mine," muttered Anna from under her jacket.

Mom's shoulders dropped, and she walked out, her long auburn hair falling along her back.

Anna used to wish she was pretty like her mother. She used to complain that it was her luck to inherit Dad's boring looks: hazel-brown eyes, wiry dark hair, freckle-specked nose. Now she hoped she would never become like her, getting over Dad so easily. Not that they have ever been a perfect family, but still. It was the heart attack that took him, but it was Mom who turned her back on the past, gave it up, like she gave away old clothes and furniture before the move to a new city.

Slowly, Anna rolled off the bed back onto her feet. She hung the jacket in the closet; ripped the tape off the box that had *GOOD CLOTHES* scribbled on its side. She unpacked and hung up her new high school uniform, and looked out of the window again.

The public park across the street looked like it might have groomed ski trails. Even if there were no groomed trails, a snow-covered walking path would do just fine. She stared out of the window for a couple of moments, then, as if obeying an irresistible call, quickly laced up her ski boots and grabbed her jacket from the closet. Poles and skis in her hands, she tiptoed to the door as quietly as the ski boots allowed. She shut the heavy steel door gently, without a sound.

The phone, the new one with that tracking app that her paranoid stepfather made her install, Anna left under her pillow.

Before she knew it, she was already out of the house, dashing across the empty snow-covered street towards the park up the hill. She didn't look back. She felt bitter and proud at once. Of course, her sneaking out like this was outrageous, but so what? The adults were too much into themselves to miss her even if she had run away for real.

The park was quiet, as if waiting for her – just a couple of parents dragging sleds with little kids, and even they were on their way out. Anna warmed up by cruising along the central alley, but there was no grip on the torn path, so she kicked off to the edge of the tree line where the snow was virgin. Under the trees it seemed darker than in the open lawn, tree trunks were hardly visible behind the falling flakes. Thick cotton-like rolls of snow weighed heavily on the birch branches and the spruce shoots.

She made a circle around the big lawn, and as she was coming on top of the hill, she felt a pleasant ache in her muscles. Down the other side of the slope stood the Park Rangers' hut, a shabby little building with a faded *AUTHORIZED ENTRY ONLY* sign across the door. The stone stairs leading to the hut were completely covered, creating a nice steep slope. Anna was tempted to glide downhill, right to the hut, but she didn't feel like climbing all the way back up the snow-covered stairs.

She stopped at the top of the hill, breathing in the cold air. The exercise made her feel better, clearing her head. She didn't even mind cleaning up her room anymore. Sneaking out was totally worth a short yelling session, but not worth being grounded, especially since the snow began to come down heavier again.

The clearing was too narrow and the slope too steep for her to smoothly turn around. She tried to execute a kick-turn by lifting one ski and pivoting on its tail, but her ski got stuck in the deep snow. Her right ankle, the one she had twisted the winter before, gave in, sending a surge of pain up her leg. The muscle twinge was so sharp that for a second she saw the stars, and the whole world around her flashed with bright colors. Anna lost her balance, instinctively jerked her foot, and crack! her binding broke off. With a pained gasp, she plopped right into the fluffy snow.

When you are into sports, you are no stranger to pain. Her coach used to say, pain is a friend who reminds you about what's real. Anna sometimes thought that as far as friends went, pain was the most reliable, because it never lied. That's why she often worked out a little too hard, making herself hurt a little too much. It made her feel certain, at least about something. That was how she busted her ankle in the first place, by training through the pain.

But she should have known better. How could something so stupid happen to her – her, a serious cross-country runner? Just a second before she was feeling so good about herself, now it gave way to furious shame. There she was, sitting in the snow, panting, not sure whether to rub her throbbing ankle or her broken ski. How could everything go wrong all at once? Anna felt hot inside, as if the pain of the twisted ankle echoed in her heart, making it ache too. For a second, it seemed tears filled her eyes, and she rubbed her face in disbelief: how pathetic would it be to cry now over a broken binding, when she managed to keep cool even at her father's funeral?

Well, at least nobody witnessed my epic fail, she thought.

"Hey, skier!" a voice said suddenly, startling her. "May I have the track?"

Usually, one hears *Track!* only if another skier is catching up, trying to pass. Anna scrambled back to her feet and quickly looked around. There was no one behind her, but several feet away under a tree stood a boy. She wasn't able to see him clearly behind the falling snow, but he looked about her age, and cute. The boy was standing up to his knees in a snow drift, his hands resting on his ski poles. Her heart jumped. A fellow skier! And they said nobody skis in the park.

"Um, sure, you can have it, but there isn't any groomed track," she replied slowly. "Everything's covered."

She picked up her broken ski, biding time. Her mind was racing, trying to come up with something to say. Preferably, something not totally lame. The last thing she wanted was him to notice her embarrassment. Her first New York City boy! It would have been cool if he asked for her number… she didn't even have her phone with her today… she didn't even know what time it was…

"Umm, you got time?" she finally asked as casually as she could manage.

The boy stepped from under the tree.

"I surely hope so." He sounded offended, as if she had asked about something private, but made no effort to even look for his phone or a watch.

The falling snow had deceived Anna. The boy was older than her, maybe a high school senior. He was tall, wide in the shoulders, had honey-blonde hair and bright blue eyes. The girls on her team would have died with envy if they saw her now. He sported tight leather pants and a fitted jacket with lots of pockets, clasps and fringes that looked more like a hand-made biker outfit than appropriate athletic gear. But that didn't matter – Anna was happy to finally meet another cross-country skier. She decided to play it cool.

"Did you lose it of something?" She rolled her eyes.

He shuddered and spoke anxiously: "It is out of order, no doubt, that I missed the track, yes, but to lose time? It is nothing like a zhom, after all... This way is unfamiliar to me, hunter..."

"What? I'm no hunter!"

"But you must be." The boy beamed, and it seemed brighter under the trees, "What is your name?"

"Anna," uttered Anna, bewildered.

"Hannah," he repeated with a sigh, as if making fun of her, but in a friendly sort of way.

Anna felt a silly smile tug at the corners of her mouth. He pronounced her name with attitude, in a kind of dignified and formal, but also really funny manner. Somehow, this boy was different, and Anna liked it.

"Greetings, Hannah!" He gave her a playful bow. "You must be a Hunter. You cannot be a Scout, because you are on skis. You seem to know your way. So, may I have your track?"

"Yeah, sure, whatever." Anna shrugged. Why did this boy insist on having her track with all the free space around? Unless, he was on some scavenger hunt with some strange rules...

"Wait," Anna squinted at him. "Scout, you mean, like, the Boy Scouts, right? Is it some kind of game?"

"Why," The stranger seemed surprised. "The Game is not on yet. Have you not been present at the last Game? Or maybe you just arrived recently... a-ah! you are new, like me! Oh, I have not yet seen such a new Hunter. And you seem so good on your skis!"

He was babbling, standing up to his knees in snow, and Anna took a moment to study him. He was lightly built, but looked strong, like he could have been a serious athlete. Most importantly, he had a very sweet and open face, the kind of face you don't want to take your eyes off. Maybe the secret was in his smile: it

Anna felt flattered that an older boy was being so friendly. It made her hot inside her chest, and for a second she worried that it would show with a treacherous blush.

shone, lighting his whole face, making his blue eyes sparkle. With his golden hair and bright eyes, he radiated warmth like a ray of sunshine.

Anna felt flattered that an older, good-looking boy was being so friendly, not arrogant or corny or full of himself like cute popular boys in her old school. It made her hot inside her chest, and for a second she worried that it would show with a treacherous blush on her cheeks. She really liked him. She knew what that meant: the more you like a boy, the less you should show it. That's what the older girls on the team were saying all the time.

"That's just great," she said indifferently, when he interrupted the stream of his speech to draw a breath, "Actually, I was on my way home."

"Oh, yes, I am going home too. I just need the track."

"Again, with the track... You might find it easier to step out of the snow drift, for starters." Anna chuckled.

He furrowed his eyebrows, visibly confused.

"Come to me." She waved her hand.

He shifted his weight, and in one imperceptible move was standing right next to her, their skis in a perfect parallel alignment. Anna glanced down at his silvery skis, and it seemed for a second that they left no trace. *No, no*, she said to herself, *The snow is just too fluffy.*

"Looks like you found your own track, right?"

"Looks like I am at-trackted to you," he replied with a disarming smile, making Anna blush. He edged closer to her, and, as he leaned forward on his poles, two neat golden braids fell on his chest. Anna has never seen a guy with such fancy long hair – that's New York City for you! She couldn't help a laugh.

"Are you a hippie?"

"No, I am Sanny!" He laughed too.

"You mean, your name is Sanny?"

He nodded.

"How appropriate," said Anna, swallowing another giggle. "Are you sure you're not a hippie?"

"Quite sure."

"Well, nice meeting you, Sanny."

"It is my honor to welcome you," he replied with enthusiasm

which surprised Anna a little, but made her like him even more. At the same time, she couldn't shake a feeling of something being weird about him. Not in a bad way, but definitely weird, as in take off your skis and go home right now kind of weird. She bent down to undo the other binding to signal that the conversation was over, when suddenly her head started to spin; instinctively, she reached out to grab on to his hand. What she didn't expect was that Sanny immediately wrapped his arm around her shoulders.

"I hope you are not thinking of removing both skis outside," he said with genuine concern in his voice. "You have been out for too long, you must go home,"

"Yeah, just about to do that," muttered Anna, freeing herself.

"Step in my track," Sanny said resolutely.

And, before Anna could understand what was happening, she was standing behind him, her ski between his skis, the tip of her boot touching his heel. She only had time to think that it was getting stupid and dangerous, when everything started to glitter in front of her eyes; it felt like the ground moved beneath her feet.

I must be dizzy, should have had a snack before running out, raced through her mind. She almost blacked out, but, all of a sudden, the spell was gone. The ground was moving for real, or rather, Anna and Sanny were sliding with a dangerous speed into the wooden door of the Park Rangers' hut, and now they were about to crash into the locked door.

"Welcome home!" exclaimed Sanny, shooting a glance at her over his shoulder.

"No way I'm going with him into this shack," thought Anna, shutting her eyes; she clutched Sanny's belt and braced for a crash.

Chapter II
in which Anna's situation starts to flesh out

here was no crash. Instead, Anna's face felt warmth. She shook her head and opened her eyes. She was standing on the threshold of a spacious room with a row of doors on each wall. Across from the entrance door there was a stone fireplace, and the fire was high. Shaggy, candy-colored fur rugs covered the floor in random patches. The arched ceiling disappeared into darkness.

How come there is so much space in this tiny old shack? And who started the fire? she wondered, glancing at her companion. He had already removed his shiny skis, and put them against the wall. They were covered with some rune-like markings, an unknown brand, probably foreign.

Anna still had her good ski attached to her boot and her broken ski in her hand. She would have panicked, if she wasn't too busy feeling ridiculous, standing there on one ski. Blushing, she stepped back into the doorway, but stumbled against the threshold. The poles and the skis crossed, and she fell stretching out on the floor. The door shut.

"I will help!" yelled Sanny. But someone's strong hands were already lifting her. Her ski binding unlatched by itself. Dropping the poles and the broken ski, Anna freed herself. In front of her stood a tall guy, perhaps as old as a college freshman, dressed in a crude leather jacket that looked hand-stitched, like Sanny's. His dark hair was braided into a long single braid. He looked Anna over; when he saw her skis on the floor, his eyebrows arched over his cherry-brown eyes. Sanny came up, and greeted him with a big hug.

"Hey, Heepi! Hannah, you asked if I am Heepi, so here he is, Heepi!"

"Sanny," said the dark-haired guy in a grave voice, his eyes shifting from Anna's face to Anna's skis. "Hunter Sanny, who is he?!"

Was this Heepi so blind that he mistook Anna for a boy? Of course, she did have a short haircut, and she was pretty athletic, but come on... Anna was about to give him some snide remark, but was distracted by Sanny, who placed his hands on her and the guy's shoulders, pushing them in a group hug.

"Heepi, this is Hannah." Sanny was all smiles, turning his face from Heepi to Anna, as if inviting the two of them to be best friends.

"Skier Sanny, how did he get into the Home?" demanded Heepi, shaking off his arm.

"On my heels."

"And the door let him through?!"

"Yes," said Sanny, no longer smiling.

"But this is a mighty shape shifter!" whispered Heepi, for some reason pointing at Anna's skis.

"No!" moaned Sanny. His sweet face reflected terror, then disgust. He quickly snatched his hand off Anna's shoulder and stepped away, like she was toxic. "And I had so much love for it... Should we call Yaret?"

"No need to bother Lord Yaret, we'll kill it ourselves," replied the one named Heepi and howled: "Zho-o-om!"

This word had the effect of opening doors in the walls, and people suddenly filled the room. They were all men no older than twenty, all dressed in leather. They all stared at her with fear and hatred. Horrified as she was, Anna couldn't help but noticing that they were all very handsome in an oddly similar way.

Her heart froze. This was it! Her last hour had come, and it was going to be horrible. On her first day in the big city she fell into some bikers gang's den. She couldn't tell if their mistaking her for a boy was bad or really bad. Mom had been right, normal people didn't ski in the park. What's worse, James had been right too – she'd got in trouble in no time.

"You won't get away with it!" She spat the first brave thing that came into her head, and picked up her ski pole, clutching it like a lance. "My stepfather is a cop! He'll arrest all of you!"

"It speaks strange words," exhaled Sanny. "Shapeshifter indeed!"

"Zhom, zhom!" the crowd was chanting.

Ski poles appeared in guys' hands. The ring was closing in around Anna. She wanted to scream, but only managed a wheeze.

"Sha, Hunters!" Someone's voice carried over the noise.

The crowd dispersed. An older man was making his way towards Anna. He wore a green snorkel parka, the same type her skiing coach had, except extremely worn out and soiled. He came close, squinting and wincing, as if with a toothache. He stretched his hand to Anna, and, for some reason, she couldn't move away. The man put his palm on Anna's forehead, pushed back slightly and looked her straight in the eyes. The eyes in his rough face were green like spring grass.

The gang boss, thought Anna. Everything was turning red before her eyes, and she clearly felt a taste of blood in her mouth from her bit lip. She was about to faint. The last thing she saw was a shiny bracelet with a jingle bell charm on his dirty wrist. Then she heard a husky voice.

"Skiers, this is not a shapeshifter wyssun."

The attackers put down their poles.

"Hunter Sanny simply brought in a very, very... well, let's just say, a very new one."

The crowd released a sigh of relief. Anna re-opened her eyes, and met Sanny's hopeful gaze.

"But, Scout Semille, his skis are so... dim!" Heepi squeamishly poked Anna's skis with his pole.

"Dim or not, this is not a wyssun," declared the man in the green parka. He bent over, picked up Anna's skis, and carefully leaned them against the wall by the front door. "And it's no zhom," he grumbled.

"Semille, could it be because of me? Have I not welcome Hannah with enough love?" asked Sanny. He rushed to Anna, and flung his arm around her shoulder.

The man in the green parka shrugged. "What do I know about love? I'm a Scout, not a Counsilor."

Just as he said that, a completely inexplicable character walked into the room. At first glance, he looked like a skinny teenage boy no taller than Anna, but there was something ancient about his smooth face. That which in the features of the others was beautiful, in his face seemed exaggerated, as if every part was taken to the extreme. His eyes were too big, his nose and mouth too small. His large, elongated ears stuck out, and his skin seemed stretched too tightly over the delicate bones. A long white mane fell over his shoulders, cascading down his back, the greenish tips of his locks blending with the metallic tunic. There was a bird-like quality in the way he cocked his head and moved his fragile body. The man bowed, and a little white fluffy animal, which apparently was hiding in his feathery shoulder pad, almost fell off his narrow shoulder. Others returned the bow with reverence.

No, this is the real leader, thought Anna.

"Counsilor Llewelys," said Heepi. "Hunter Sanny brought a new one, his skis are dim."

"Hunter brings one human, true." The way he spoke was melodic and yet somewhat strained, like he was making an effort to come up with the words.

"I thought Hannah is a new Hunter..." Sanny's voice trailed off.

"Scout verifies one human, true," the white-haired man continued, half-closing his enormous almond-shaped eyes. His irises were like iridescent glass marbles.

"True. Counsilor Llewelys, it is a juvenile female," responded the man in the green parka.

For a moment, the pale Counsilor studied Anna with a tiny frozen smile that made him appear bored and amused at the same time.

At first glance, he looked like a skinny teenage boy no taller than Anna,
but there was something ancient about his smooth face.

"Skiers," he finally announced, "The Rules of the Seventh Approximation stipulate: If one human comes, it stays until it becomes. If one Skier brings one human, the human stays until it leaves. True." Having uttered this, he turned on his heels and made his exit through the front door.

The fellow in the green parka looked around, glanced at Anna, shook his head, muttering something like, "Here we go again...", and walked out through a door to the right. Others quietly put away their ski poles, and departed as well. In a minute only a few guys were left. They dispersed around the room, patting each other on the backs and chatting, like old friends catching up. Everybody seemed to be minding their own business. Apparently, they were not interested in Anna anymore.

Anna, who was frozen in shock all this time, felt like she just caught a break. Still, all her instincts screamed to get out of this strange place as soon as possible.

"Skiers, I did not understand, Llewelys called Hannah something," Sanny said in his clear voice, "Who-man... something – what was that?"

"Counsilor Llewelys said new one," replied Heepi from the corner.

"No, he said something else," insisted Sanny.

"Sanny, what Counsilors say is not of our understanding. It is enough to know that Hannah is not a shapeshifter. He is a Skier like us, and he is welcome in this Home." Heepi smiled at Anna, and everybody looked at her, nodding with friendly smiles.

"Oh, Hannah, it is wonderful that you are not a shapeshifter!" Sanny squeezed Anna's shoulders.

Yeah, wonderful, thought Anna. *Definitely, a gang of lunatics, or maybe even a cult.*

"It's great," she agreed out loud, forcing her lips into a smile.

"As for your skis, with some love they shall glow like they should. I will help you with everything." Sanny took her hand in his, and stroked it.

He was gazing at her tenderly, and his big blue eyes were radiating happiness. Amidst all this chaos, he was like a bright ray of sunshine. Anna's heart skipped a beat – she couldn't help but liking him. How stupid was that? She shook her head, freed herself from Sanny's warm embrace and took a couple of careful steps toward the door.

A tall dark-skinned guy was sitting on the rug, blocking her way. He seemed absorbed in fixing one of the many long braids decorating his head.

"What's with the braids?" muttered Anna and immediately regretted it, because the guy lifted his lively brown eyes at her and winked.

"Well, we are no Counsilors to wear hair loose, are we!" He said, and burst into laughter, flashing impossibly white teeth. In a moment everybody caught up, and the sound of laughter filled the room.

"Oh, you, Omónie, you said it," moaned Heepi, wiping away tears.

Taking advantage of the momentary distraction, she jumped over Omónie's outstretched legs and rushed to the door, but he swiftly caught her by the elbow. Realizing, she was no match for him, Anna went limp.

"Are you going already?" There was no threat in Omónie's voice, but his friendliness still made her shudder.

"Well...um, I'd like to..."

"Ah... I hoped you would stay, sing with us."

"I have to go!" she squeaked.

"Oh, you know how that makes me feel!" cried Omónie with comic reproach. "This is how!"

Before Anna could say anything, Omónie quickly dug into a small leather pouch attached to his belt, and pulled out a palm-size furry creature, the size of a small guinea pig.

Except it wasn't a guinea pig or a rat, or anything Anna had ever seen before. Its short gleaming fur was electric pink, making the creature look like a spool of cotton candy – that is if a spool of cotton candy had an animal muzzle with a single eye above a little trunk of a nose. Without hesitation, Omónie shoved the little creature into Anna's hands.

"It's pink!" screamed Anna, holding the little furry thing as far as possible.

"Exactly! Now only a song will make me feel better!"

The creature wrinkled its nose and blinked its eye.

"And, it's one-eyed!" Anna couldn't believe what she was seeing.

"Sure it is, it is a sub. We are no Counsilors to keep oglies, are we," said Omónie, and everybody burst into laughter again. Obviously, he was considered very witty by the rest of this strange gang.

"A song! A song!" shouted Omónie. Suddenly Heepi carried a tune over the laughter, and his voice sounded unexpectedly pleasant, like the voice of a trained singer. The rest immediately joined. It was a peculiar song with a melody rhythmical and plaintive at the same time, like nothing Anna had ever heard before. They sang:

Where no color's to be seen
In pitch black the paths begin.
Red ignites the game of life
For a hunter to arrive.
Merry with an orange hue
A Hunter's heart is feeling new.
The mind is shining yellow-bright,
It gains the power of insight,
Understanding ever clear
The Hunter, green inside the mirror.
Upside down above the blue
Only a pure mind is true.
Shows the deepest indigo
Where a ready soul will go.
The Game's played out without regret,
The Hunter wraps in violet,
Seeing in the light of power
That, like snow, truth has no color.

For a moment Anna fell under a spell, her gaze moving from face to face, which seemed more and more beautiful as the boys kept singing. All of them looked like they could have come from different parts of the world, yet all were handsome in a similar, otherworldly way: graceful, with precise small features, high cheekbones and radiant eyes. Also, all had very long, well-groomed hair, braided in a variety of styles.

So, this is where all the gorgeous guys are, passed through Anna's mind. *They all join cult gangs.*

In the meantime, the little creature Anna was holding started to tickle her palm. It brought her back to her senses.

Why am I still here?! she thought in terror, and backed to the door without taking her eyes off of the singing boys. No one seemed to pay any attention to her. Just as she reached the door, she bumped into someone. It was that older man in the green parka, the one who they called Scout Semille. He was standing by the door, leaning against the frame. His face was weather-beaten and wrinkled, and his intense green eyes looked out of place on his face, like a priceless emerald ring on the dirty finger of a homeless panhandler.

"You can't leave," he said, shaking his head. Anna sized him up, figuring, he was in no shape to stop her. He looked like a regular middle-aged guy, actually, a little worse than a regular guy. He met her stare, grinned, and gently removed the furry animal from her hands.

Anna flushed red with anger, and said firmly, "Watch me."

She ducked under his arm. He didn't try to stop her. Anna cast a final glance at the singing Sanny, pushed the door open and jumped out.

Chapter III
in which Anna
plays with fire

nna was standing on the threshold of the same room. Nothing had changed. But she was sure she had just stepped out! She jumped behind the door again. Again, she was standing in the doorway, facing the fireplace.

"But I just left!" she cried in a panic, her voice carrying over the singing.

"You can't leave!" Semille shouted back.

Anna rushed behind the door once again, wishing more than anything not to see any more of the weird crowd. Now she was standing in an empty room.

"You still haven't gone anywhere," said the familiar husky voice. The Scout squatted in front of the fireplace. The fire was dying. It was the same room, now empty.

That was too much. Her legs buckled in underneath her, and she dropped to her knees, clutching her chest with both hands.

"Praying won't help," said Semille, "You may enter on someone else's heels, but you have to exit on your own, understand?"

"I don't understand anything! I still don't know where I am... First you can't wait to get rid of me, now I can't leave... those weird songs and dumb jokes... speaking in puzzles... What kind of people are you?"

"Not kind." Scout shrugged. "Not people, either."

"Are you... an alien from another planet?" Anna shuddered.

"Do I look like an alien? Sheesh!" Semille shook his messy head.

"Who, then?"

"Can't you see? We're Skiers."

"Right, so am I..."

"I told you, not people. Same planet, different world. Wyssun World. Different tasks. Take the Hunters. Their task is to hunt wyssun."

"Hunt who?"

"Not who, what. Wyssuns are monsters. They're everywhere, and they can look like anything. The creature Omónie showed you, that was a wyssun, albeit the harmless pocket pet. They feed on love, see."

"Well, I'm pretty sure I've never seen anything like that before."

"Oh, you've seen them, you just never paid attention." Semille grinned at her, as if letting her in on a secret. "I told you, they're everywhere. They've got to be hunted, or they'll overrun the world."

"Which world?"

"Any world."

Anna took a moment to think. She was not the kind of girl who daydreams about wandering into fairyland, or being beamed up to an alien spaceship. She never thought of herself as someone with a great imagination: her greatest fantasy was going to the Winter Olympics, which as far as she was concerned was as fantastical as going to the Land of Oz. But Dorothy never excepted to find herself in Oz either.

"Let me get this clear," she said thoughtfully. "Am I in some kind of parallel world?"

"You are in the Wyssun World. I suppose it's parallel to some, just as it's perpendicular to others."

"How is this possible?"

"How is anything possible?" He shrugged again. "I don't know. I'm no Counsilor."

"So, you're a Hunter?"

"No, I'm a Scout, an investigator, a go-between the worlds. Why do you think I can talk to you with ease? It's 'cause I know

Sometimes, the way back is forward, just like, sometimes, the way forward is backwards.

how to talk to people. The Hunters can't. Didn't you get it, they cannot see that you are a human girl. They think, not being a shapeshifter is good enough."

"Why would they think I'm some kind of shapeshifter?"

"Because you look just like them, but feel different. Shapeshifters also look just like people, except they're not really alive. They feel dead inside, understand? Disgusting! That's why the Hunters were ready to, you know, do away with you."

Anna wrinkled her nose in indignation. How could anyone mistake her, a nice fourteen-year-old girl, for some kind of living dead?

"If anyone looks dead inside, it would be that freaky elf."

"We don't use the e-word around here, pet." Semille waved his hands in comic horror. "They call themselves Alva. But here in the Wyssun World if you see an Alva, you may address him as Counsilor."

"Councilor, like he's on a council, or Counselor, like a school counselor?" Anna made sure to spill enough sarcasm in her voice. She wasn't really trying to be mean to this weird man in dirty clothes, she just wanted to show him that she could see through his outlandish lies.

"Well, Counsilors do offer counsel, and they are on the Council, so, you can say, it's both." Apparently, he took her wisecracking seriously.

She was right about something for a change: the space-alien-elf was the one in charge.

"The Counsilor said, the human stays until it leaves. That means, I can leave, right?"

"Right."

She dashed to the front door, slamming her body into it. It didn't budge. She wanted to pull it, but there was no doorknob. In fact, none of the doors had doorknobs of any kind.

"I'm stuck! I can't go back!" she slammed her hand on the door, forgetting all caution.

"Can't or won't?" Semille squinted his eyes at Anna, studying her with what seemed like concern, and shook his head. "Besides, sometimes, the way back is forward, just like, sometimes, the way forward is backwards. Keep searching. Ways change, we keep up. It is the Rule of the Seventh Approximation."

"Is this Approximation your law?"

The Scout stopped smiling, straightened his back, spat on his palm and smoothed his messy hair. Then he looked around and uttered with reverence:

"The Seventh Approximation is the Way of the Soil."

"Right. So what are you... approximating?"

"Ah, you wouldn't understand even if I told you."

"Why don't you lie to me, isn't that what adults do when they don't know what to say?" Anna said bitterly.

"Ha! That's a good one. See, we don't lie. Can't. Not in our function." Semille spread his arms in mock regret.

Anna vaguely remembered something about magical creatures not being able to lie, but she wasn't sure what the fairy tales said. She had never been an eager reader, and especially, not a fan of fantasy books. At school none of her friends were video-game nerds or were into comics. The girls on the ski team seemed to be more interested in boys – or rather talking about boys, because, as far as she knew, none of her girlfriends had kissed a boy.

Now, she regretted not paying more attention to magical tales, because it surely looked like she had just ended up in one.

"All right," she said. "If you must tell the truth, please tell me, how do I get home?"

"In order to ask properly, you have to know exactly what your home is. Do you?"

Anna hung her head. The truth was, she didn't know what her home was anymore. With Dad gone, their house in Michigan was no longer the place she remembered as home she'd grown up in, and James' apartment in an old New York brownstone building didn't feel like a home at all.

Semille noticed her hesitation, and gave her a comforting pat on the shoulder.

"Anyway, what's the rush? You were at-trackted; you didn't cross by accident."

"I didn't mean to, it just happened." Anna blushed. "I'm sorry."

"Oh, no, don't be sorry, be glad. Nothing just happens. If the Door opened one way, perhaps, it may open the other way too. There's still a chance you won't turn any time soon."

On that cryptic note, Semille abruptly got up and went to one of the doors.

"Turn what?" Anna asked quickly. "Turn what?!" she screamed after him, but he slipped past the door and was gone. Then Anna was alone.

She looked around, for the first time trying to pay attention to her surroundings. It struck her that everything in the room looked slightly off, as if it had been hand-made without any particular idea or plan, or even grew by itself. The fireplace seemed to be thoughtlessly carved into the corner. The doors, which numbered seven counting the front entrance, were all different sizes, and spaced unevenly. The soft fur rugs covering the stone floor were stitched together without any consideration of shade and shape. There was not a single straight line to be found. Everything was crooked, yet, strangely enough, appeared quite pleasant to the eye. She didn't want to admit it, but Anna felt cozy and comfortable in this unusual room, and it even occurred to her that maybe there was a logic to it after all, but a logic she couldn't understand.

"I envy your belief in me." A voice made her jump to her feet. It was a squeaky, toy kind of voice.

"Who's there?"

"Knock, knock, who's there?" The voice mocked her.

Anna cocked her head and listened in.

"There must be someone else alive in this town," the voice continued. It seemed to be coming out of the fireplace.

"Talking fire, that's what I need," muttered Anna. She walked over to the fireplace and cautiously peeked in. It seemed, behind the low flames there was the face of a little animal. Suddenly a ball of fire leaped out of the fireplace right onto the rug. Anna jumped away. The ball unfolded, and turned into a shaggy fiery-orange creature with a dark muzzle and paws. It started fussing around her, snorting and chortling. At least this one had both eyes in place.

"Did you just talk?" Anna inquired.

The animal sat on its haunches and said, "It's on!"

"What's on?"

"Oh, it's on," squeaked the creature, leaping about the room.

Maybe he is trying to tell me something, reasoned Anna. I just need to ask the right questions.

"Who are you?"

"Knock, knock," squeaked the animal, rolling on the rug.

"Silly animal…"

"I know you are, but what am I," replied the creature.

"Are you messing with me?" Her reflexes sharpened by anger, Anna jumped at the offender, and quickly grabbed it. The little thing trembled in her hands, tickling her palms and squealing.

"Where is the exit?" demanded Anna, giving the creature a firm shake. Maybe he reacts to certain words, she thought, and yelled: "Door? Door!"

"Doors are open, fences down," recited the creature. Anna looked at the front door, but it remained closed. The creature went on, "Which of them will be the one?"

The little body in Anna's hands started to get warmer: the creature was heating up. In a second, it became too hot to hold onto. She opened her hands, and the little red thing swiftly jumped to the floor and back into the fireplace.

Already in the fire, it looked back at Anna, and said clearly, "Back and forth, gain and loss, any threshold can be crossed," and dissolved in the orange fire.

Anna rushed to the fireplace, but the little monster was gone. She sat down on the rugs, and took a moment to think.

All right, she said to herself. *It was teasing me, but it also confirmed that there is an exit. The Scout guy said the same thing, that I must simply search for the way out. So, before the others come back, I should try one door at a time.*

She summoned all her strength, got up from the floor, walked up to the nearest door to the right from the fireplace, and pushed it.

Chapter IV
in which Anna's mind
is blown

harp screams of birds, cold bright light, and piercing wind attacked her senses. Suddenly Anna was standing on the edge of a high precipice. Far down below lead waves were crashing against the rocks. Beyond the foamy line of the surf all the way to the horizon lay the wintry sea. A strong wind from the sea was pushing long torn clouds behind her back. She followed them with her eyes and saw far back in the distance snowy cliffs, dissolving into the low sky. Above her head large sea birds were ripping through the air. All around her stretched a rocky field covered with damp snow, with nothing in it but thorny bushes with small yellow flowers shaking in the wind. The plateau abruptly ended at the sea side.

Anna felt the icy wind chill her to her bones. She turned back: behind her there was a low dugout with a weathered wooden door. Shme true – she found herself in the room. With a moan of relief she ran up to the fireplace. As her shivering subsided, Anna looked around and realized that the room was much smaller. Also, she was not alone. A hunched figure sat in the corner, wrapped in a faded yellow cloak. The man sat with his head hung low, so that his long braids fell over his clasped fingers onto the floor. He didn't move when Anna approached.

"Ahem, excuse me," she started politely. "I have just stepped out to somewhere, like, a sea shore of some kind. But it's not what I need. Could you please tell me which door to try?"

The man ignored her.

"Please!" begged Anna, "I can't find the way on my own!"

The man lifted his head and glanced over Anna with uncaring eyes.

"Why don't you help me?"

"Get away," he said hoarsely.

Anna stepped back.

"You don't have to be rude..."

"Get away, young one. I released my wyssun. I have no feelings for you." He rose, and the yellow cloak fell on the ground, giving Anna a chance to look at him, and making her gasp.

His once fancy leather garment was ragged. His face had the same handsome features like all the others, but was worn-out, tired and empty, like a young man ravaged by a horrible premature aging inside and out. Looking at him made Anna deeply sad to the point of anger, the way she felt a lot since the heart attack took Dad. It was as if something once nice and good was ruined beyond repair, and she was helpless to do anything about it. At this moment, she really hated the stranger, as if it upsetting her was his intention.

With a heavy sigh the man dragged himself over to the smaller one of the two doors. He pushed it, and she leaned forward, trying to get a glimpse of what was behind it. He stepped into the darkness, and Anna lungs filled up with cold air that smelled like ashes. Just as the thought crossed her mind that this was probably a door she should avoid, she felt a strong push, like a sudden gust of wind shoved her in the back. She stumbled across the threshold and heard the door slam behind her.

"No!" she screamed, and tried to get back in, but there was no handle or knob to grab, just a solid stone wall. Anna scratched at the wall, but to no avail.

"Help! Somebody, please!" She shouted, but not even an echo answered her.

She was completely alone in the dank darkness. The strain of her recent adventure finally took a toll on Anna, and she slid down, crouching against the wall. She was cold, tired, and her feet were uncomfortable in her ski boots. There was no way of knowing how much time she had already spent in this bizarre Wyssun World, nor how much time had passed back at home. Mom must be freaking out, or worse, James must be freaking out too, calling a full police search for her. That was the last thing she needed, proving them right, that she was just a dumb kid who didn't know any better. With a sad sigh, she hugged her knees.

Suddenly, a faint light pierced the cold darkness, as if someone had turned on a small lantern. A dim glow coming from an orb the size of a softball, which seemed to be made of glass, illuminated a tall figure. The figure was wrapped in a ragged cloak, and barely visible in the soft yellow light. Anna couldn't make out the face, but immediately decided that it was the aged Hunter. So, he changed his mind and returned to help her!

"You are in a baaad Way," whispered the man, drawing out his vowels. His voice sounded different from before, more playful than grumpy, like he was putting up a show while trying hard not to smile.

"No kidding!" cried Anna. "Can you show me the way out?"

"Oh, I could show you the Way. What will you offer in return?"

Anna dug through her ski jacket's pockets. She had no phone on her, no watch. In her mad dash out of the house she hadn't even taken her wallet with her. Her skis and poles were back at the first room. All she had was her beanie hat and a pair of ski gloves.

"Would a hat or the gloves be of any use?" she offered.

"I have no use for a hat, and I already own a pair of gloves," replied the man.

"Could you please help me anyway? I'm sorry I've got nothing to offer you!"

"Oh, you've got something," ignoring her plea, the man continued in his creepy, smiling whisper. "You are young. Likely, innocent. Possibly, unkissed. Are you, now?"

"What... that's gross! And none of your business," she said defiantly, indignation overcoming despair.

"If I open a door for you, will you trade me a kiss?"

"No way!" Anna leapt to her feet, and had to lean against the cold wall to fight a sudden queasiness. "Why would you ask for something like that anyway? Didn't you just say you have no feelings for me?"

"I said no such thing." He let out a soft chuckle. "But I accept your choice."

The glowing ball fell out of his arms and rolled on the ground until it hit a wall to the right of her. In its dim light, Anna could see a narrow outline of a door. Without even thanking the cloaked man, Anna rushed to the door and slammed her whole body's weight at it. The door opened and she fell back into the welcoming warmth of the fireplace room.

That was close, thought Anna, hugging herself to contain a shiver. *At least this one didn't try to kill me. But he didn't mistake me for a boy, that's for sure,* she said to herself, twisting a strand of short hair at the back of her head. She couldn't tell which was worse.

The man was mumbling something about a kiss. Why on Earth would she ever want to kiss some old creep? Now, of course, if Sanny asked her for a kiss, that would be completely different. Sanny was special. He definitely was worthy of her first kiss.

"Hannah! Here you are! I am so glad."

Standing by the door was Sanny with his bright smile, sparkling eyes and golden braids. He had his skis under his arm.

"Sanny!" Anna gasped. "I was just thinking about you."

"I could tell." Sanny leaned his glowing skis against the wall, walked to Anna and got a hold of her hands.

"Oh, your hands are cold." And he began to rub Anna's fingers gently. No, there was no way Sanny thought of her as just another buddy.

"You wouldn't believe what happened to me," she said. "I walked out through that door to some sea shore…"

"I believe you. You describe the Cape. How did you pull yourself there? It is not the season for the capers yet."

"Season for who?"

"*If I open a door for you, will you trade me a kiss?*"

"*No way!*"

"Those wyssun living in the sea by the Cape," explained Sanny, clearly happy for an opportunity to display his experience. He let go of her hands.

"Whatever." Anna shrugged, thinking that she'd rather kept her hands in his. "And when I came back, there was this gloomy... Hunter. He was rude to me! He went into some dark room." She waved her hand towards the scary door.

"It must have been Alokee who is departing soon."

"He said, he doesn't have feelings for me." Anna rolled her eyes.

"He has no love left in him."

Sanny uttered those words with particular sadness, and hung his head. For a moment, Anna contemplated whether to tell Sanny the rest of the story, about the old man's disturbing request for a kiss, but then she decided against it. This conversation was taking a turn too important to miss. So, she held her breath for a bit, and asked an important question:

"Do you? I mean, love anybody?"

"Me? Why, I love everybody! And you – the most!" He stepped closer to Anna and wrapped his arms around her in a tender embrace. Being so close to him made her dizzy. Her heart pounded so loudly she could hardly hear him speak.

"Hannah," Sanny continued in a heartfelt voice, "I am so happy you arrived. Now you are the youngest, and the most loved. I used to be the youngest, now I move on. Hannah, we shall go on the next hunt together, you may go on my heels. When I was the youngest, I was taken to my first hunt by Omónie. You should know, Omónie is so strong! You would never believe that he arrived right before me. Such a great Hunter! He faced off with shapeshifters in a zhom several times, yet he has never lost any time!"

Sanny got carried away and waved his arms in excitement. Out of his embrace, Anna regained her senses. She was still stuck in a bizarre place, listening to words which made no sense. The first two doors she tried so far had taken her to places even further away from home, probably, deeper in danger. And now Sanny brought up this word again – zhom – the same word the

Hunters were chanting when they almost killed her.

"Wait, Sanny, what's a zhom?"

"A zhom happens when in the subway tunnel during a hunt a strong wyssun resists the will of the Hunter. There can be only one of two outcomes: either the Hunter overpowers the wyssun or the wyssun overpowers the Hunter. If the wyssun prevails and consumes the body – nothing can help, the Hunter is gone. But if the body is rescued, the time is taken off, and the Hunter will be back."

Sanny obviously enjoyed his new role as a mentor. His cheeks were glowing and his long eyelashes trembling with excitement.

"What do you mean, take off time?" asked Anna, trying to pay attention. It was hard not to get distracted by Sanny's sweet face. Even the silliest things he was saying came out adorable. She had never felt this way about any boy.

"Well, you know, one has only so much time. After the time is taken off the Hunter will wear out sooner, there will remain less love in him, but he will be able to hunt again."

"So, how much time do they take off?"

"Oh, this is up to the Council to decide," Sanny pronounced in a solemn voice.

"Interesting." Anna scoffed. "So, you get wounded, then take off some time and hop! as good as new! I wish we all had it this way."

Sanny frowned at her.

"Why would we all wish for it? We do not wish it at all! A zhom is a terrible thing to happen. But do not fret, Hannah, it is unlikely to happen on a first hunt. When you are on track with an older, stronger Hunter..."

"On track, that's how you brought me here," guessed Anna.

"Yes. You leave your skis at Home and step on mine. They will take us to the place of the hunt."

"In the subway!" She grinned in disbelief.

"In the subway, surely not in the woods." Sanny nodded. "The subway wyssun are the most abundant. Well, the capers present a good challenge too, also the alleys... but, the tunnels simply crawl with wyssun."

"So, do you run down the rails, or what?"

Sanny nodded again.

"I see. Now I know why the trains stop in the tunnels," Anna said sarcastically.

Sanny blue eyes widened.

"You are so perceptive!" There was sincere admiration in his voice. "When I first arrived, I did not even suspect about The Danger of Disclosure."

"Wait, what now, danger of what?"

"Disclosure. It is when everything is revealed."

"And that's dangerous how?" inquired Anna, suppressing laughter.

"I do not know how to explain," Sanny said with a humble bow. "But the Counsilors say, *As the world is about to end, everything is revealed.*"

"And what in the world do trains have to do with it?"

"I do not understand trains myself either, none of the Hunters I know have ever seen trains," Sanny continued apologetically. "Semille says trains are a figure of speech, I am not sure what he means. But the Counsilors say that when trains stop, it violates the order of things. Everything that is out of order creates a Danger of Disclosure. Oh, it is much worse than a zhom!"

Sanny put his fingers into the pouch on his hip, quickly glancing inside.

"Yes, I am terribly afraid of it," he declared, closing the pouch.

While Anna enjoyed being close to Sanny and listening to the sound of his voice, she found the whole conversation very confusing and a bit annoying. Especially, since Sanny was no longer holding her.

"I don't know how I feel about this," she said irritably.

"Oh, Hannah, how could I forget!" exclaimed Sanny, slapping himself in the forehead. "You do not know who you feel because you have no pocket wyssun of your own yet! Sure, they sap you a little, but a Hunter has love to spare. Here, look at mine!"

Sanny dug in the belt pouch and produced a small multicolored animal. It was similar to the weird gerbil Omónie threw at her, except Sanny's pet had pale blue skin. For the first time she had a chance to look at the thing closely.

Although by now Anna has seen several strange things and people, she couldn't help a gasp of astonishment. There was nothing normal about the pocket wyssun. It had an upright pear-shaped fat body, small enough to fit into Anna's palm, but heavy as lead.

The head was topped with a pair of widely set triangular, slightly translucent ears. Between the ears sat a single bright blue eye, framed by fluffy lashes. The creature had a tiny elephant trunk instead of a nose, and seemingly no mouth at all. It did, however, have a long rat-like tail, pink like its trunk, and tiny monkey paws.

"I never knew something can be cute and gross at the same time," she muttered in awe.

"You cannot go without a pocket wyssun, otherwise how you will know your true feeling?" said Sanny.

"Oh, I don't know, maybe just by feeling them?"

"Nobody can do that!" Sanny laughed. "You may feel gratitude, while it is really shame, or you feel courage, while it is really fear. That is why we have pocket wyssuns. A pocket wyssun changes color when a Skier's feelings change. When a Skier has a feeling, he looks at his wyssun, and knows for sure what kind of feeling it is. When you know your feelings, your mind is pure, and, as the Counsilors say, *We must have our minds pure as we are pure minds.*"

Anna tickled the little animal behind the ear. The wyssuns fur was now predominantly lavender, with flashes of turquoise and gold.

"So, what am I feeling?"

"I would not know. My wyssun only shows my feelings."

"So, what does it mean you're feeling?"

"Love, what else." Sanny smiled. "With a touch of hope and fear."

Anna blushed. It was very exciting to hear Sanny say the word love again. She really wanted to talk more about it, but felt embarrassed that Sanny would think of her as too eager. That was the lesson Anna learned from the older girls on her ski team: never show a boy you like him, and most importantly, never say it first. So, although she liked Sanny a whole lot, she shrugged indifferently, and changed the subject.

"This isn't the same as the Counsilor had," she remarked, caressing the soft fur. "That one was all white."

"Ah! The Counsilor has an oglie wyssun."

"What, the Counsilors don't have any feelings?" Anna chuckled.

"No, not the way we do." Sanny pursed his lips. "In any case," he lowered his voice in a trusting tone, "The subs are more to my liking."

"So what kind do the Scouts have?" asked Anna, thinking of Semille.

"They cannot keep wyssuns because they cross back and forth through the veil. It would be dangerous to take a wyssun across. They have no skis either. But the Scouts have the jingle bells."

"What for?"

"Well, as Semille himself told me, *When you become overwhelmed by reality, ring the bell to be reminded of what's real.*"

Sanny did such a good job imitating Semille's mysterious manner, that Anna burst into laughter.

"Yeah, that he's a good-for-nothing street bum, that's what's real," she said unkindly.

Sanny gave her a look of pity.

"Hannah." His voice was serious. "You are saying that which is not true. It is your ill memory. When I first arrived, I too was remembering things which are not true. Horrible, ugly things. But Omónie explained to me that it is the ill memory. It happens to all new Hunters, and it always goes away. Omónie's has gone away. Mine has gone away. So will yours. Do not allow it to enter your mind. Better think about us going to your first hunt together!" He beamed, and squeezed Anna's shoulder.

"All decked out in many colors, she is going on a hunt," a squeaky voice came out of the fire place.

"There!" screamed Anna, "That creature talked to me."

"Ah," Sanny waved his hand dismissively, "It is a flame

wyssun, never mind it, it always speaks nonsense."

"He sounded like he knew what he was talking about."

"No, he never does. The flamer is a mocker. He listens to conversations without understanding and later repeats without any sense. There are plenty of those in every Home. This one is not even the same one which talked to you before, because we are in a different Home, see?"

Sanny swung his hand around in a wide gesture. "This Home is old," he added reverently.

Indeed, the room looked smaller and shabbier compared to the first Home she saw, the one in the park, back in New York where her Mom, no doubt, was going crazy looking for her.

"I really have to get back to that room where I left my skis," said Anna, feeling a wave of anxiety come over her. "How are we going to do it?"

"We both will step on my skis and run through, how else." Sanny stroked her shoulder. "Do not fret, I will take you by the fastest Way possible."

He walked to the corner where his silvery skis leaned against the wall, laid the them on the floor with great care and stepped on. With a now familiar sense of surprise, Anna noted that as Sanny placed his feet on the skis, they stuck without any visible bindings.

"Well, get on track!" he said, looking back at her over the shoulder. His long shiny braids flapped against his back, and he smiled so brightly that Anna could not refuse. She stepped on the tails of his skis.

"Hold me tight," whispered Sanny, and Anna wrapped her arms around his narrow waist, her head spinning from being so close to him.

It seemed, they moved without moving. The door which had opened into a cold seashore before, opened into a light so blinding, that Anna had to shut her eyes.

Chapter V
in which Anna
sees a Skier in his element

Anna opened her eyes and rubbed them in disbelief. She was standing behind Sanny on the steep slope of a glacier above a deep valley. Everywhere the eye could see lay magnificent mountains. Towering peaks were covered with ancient snow, but Anna didn't feel cold. Maybe, it was the warmth of Sanny's body she was pressing against. She looked around in awe.

The sun was high in the blinding azure sky, and the jagged ridges sparkled like diamonds, rimmed by deep purple shadows in the ravines. Gold and pink reflections played off the steep soaring peaks. Soft, breathing clouds filled the valleys. Far in the distance, behind the clouds, stood a high-walled city. The windowless buildings climbed on top of one another with sharp square angles, and to Anna they looked like a pile of cardboard boxes. She strained her eyes and made out rows of narrow flags on tall poles around a citadel. Thin ribbons of smoke were raising from the roofs here and there. There were definitely people living here.

"What's there?" Anna pointed in the distance.

"Mountains – here, there, everywhere," muttered Sanny as he gave his skis a quick check; responding to his touch, surges of light flashed under his fingers, making the runic markings light up.

"No! There, can't you see? It's shaped differently! It's a city!"

"You are thinking of things which are not real. Hannah, do not let your ill memory distract you. It is all mountains, differently shaped mountains. We are in the mountains, here we hunt mountain wyssun."

"Is it going to show my moods?"

"No." Sanny laughed softly. "A mountain wyssun would never fit in a pouch. It is taller than me, has long arms and menacing claws, and its shaggy fur does not change color."

Now it was Anna's turn to laugh. "What you describe is the Abominable Snowman!"

"You are right, they are abominable. It is amazing, some wyssuns have a single big eye, others – big feet. The silent sea wyssuns with long necks live forever under water, they outlive us, Hunters. The talking ones live in fire, but only for as long as the fire is high. Some look like trees, others – just like us. It never stops surprising me." Sanny's eyes glazed. "You know, Semille sometimes jokes that we live in the Wyssun World, not the other way around."

"Don't you ever wonder, where they come from?"

"Why, I know where they come from. They cross into our world from a next world. Our world is filled with love. The wyssuns are devoid of love, so they feed on it. If they are too many, they will drain it all and ruin our world. Then, they will break through the veils and ruin other worlds as well. The loveless monsters can ruin everything. So we hunt them. But not right now," he added brightly. "Now we just slide! Hold on!"

And he pushed down.

The wind and snow rushed in Anna's face. Sanny was making skillful turns, as if he'd been practicing extreme Telemark skiing all his life. As they fell down the pristine, untouched surface of the glacier, Anna held Sanny as tightly as she could, trying to mirror the swift movements of his body, as if the two of them were dancing some frantic dance in a close embrace. It could have been romantic, if they weren't tearing downhill, as if shot out of a cannon, with fountains of snow powder sparkling in their wake.

Sanny was laughing with joy, and Anna was screaming with terror. Their crazy ride was more like a free fall, and the only thought in Anna's mind was: "Hope we don't start an avalanche!"

Yet, she didn't fall off his skis at full speed, her legs didn't give in, not did her sense of balance betray her – Anna mentally thanked her coach's brutal training for her athletic skill. When the ride was over, she was still alive, and they were standing at the end of the glacier's tongue in front of a narrow crack, just wide enough for one skinny person to pass.

"Whoosh! That was fun!" Sanny laughed, and slid in, with Anna in tow.

After the dazzling brightness of the snow, Anna for a second went blind in the dark cave. She only heard a door open and close. Next thing she knew, she crashed on the soft green rug in front of the familiar fireplace. It was the same room she had first come into. Her skis stood against the wall in the corner where Semille had put them before.

"Don't ever do that again!" Anna shouted at him. "You could have killed us both!"

Sanny smiled, shaking his head: "No, Hannah, a little slide cannot kill a Skier!"

"I don't feel too good," she whimpered, rubbing her wet face with her hands.

"You cannot know that." Sanny was still standing on his skis. "You need a pocket wyssun to truly know how you feel. Let us get you one. Step on your skis."

With a moan, Anna rose to her feet. She grabbed her skis, threw them on the rug, and poked them with her foot; the damaged binding clanked pathetically.

"See, they're broken."

Sanny's smooth cheeks blushed, and a mixture of compassion and embarrassment reflected in his bright blue eyes.

"Skis are not made, they are gifted. That which is not made cannot be broken, that which is gifted cannot be returned. Sorry to say, Hannah, but you do not love them enough, that is why they are so dim. Unloved skis will not carry you."

"Then how am I supposed to go hunting with you?"

"I guess, you can ride with me again. This is not how my first hunt was, but we can try."

"Which door are we taking?" asked Anna business-like.

That which is not made cannot be broken,
that which is gifted cannot be returned.

It seemed much safer to try new doors with Sanny by her side. Anything seemed like more fun with him.

"Which do you feel like?"

She had already tried the nearest door to the right of the fireplace, and that didn't work out too well. She came over to the next door on the right wall and pushed it. The door didn't budge.

"Sometimes doors stay closed. It means, this is not the Way out," explained Sanny. "Try another."

She nudged the third door with her palm. It seemed to give a little.

"How about this one?"

Sanny lined up his glowing skis and faced the door, turning his back to Anna. "Hold me," said Sanny, and she obediently stepped on the skis behind his back, her hands on his waist. Sanny moved, and Anna clutched his belt. The door opened and closed, and darkness swallowed them.

It smelled of iron and burned rubber. Anna was pretty sure it was a closed space. She pressed herself tightly against Sanny's back and felt his firm and warm body. Touching him felt much less awkward now, after the glacier.

"I am stepping on a rail," reported Sanny.

Suddenly a soft light came from under their feet, and ran forward as a long slim beam, splitting the darkness ahead. Sanny's silvery skis blended with the beam. As Anna's eyes grew accustomed to the low light, she realized they were in some corridor with round walls, a ceiling covered with cables and wires, railroad ties on the floor, and two steel rails across them. Everything was dusty and greasy. The only source of light was the rail Sanny and Anna were hovering over. It appeared that some glowing force field generated between the two skis and the rail, allowing Sanny and Anna to slide down the rail with ease.

"...it is always dark in the tunnel at first, but when you find the rail, the skis give you light," whispered Sanny. "I will be searching for the wyssun track now. Try to feel its presence"

Anna realized that they began to move. The sensation reminded her of when Sanny dragged her into the shack in the park, the same dizziness and glittering, motion without moving.

Time stopped. She felt like an antenna receiving invisible waves. Suddenly she heard a loud noise – a train passed by. They really were in a subway tunnel!

"Do not get distracted by the trains of thought, they exist only in your mind," Sanny said quietly.

Anna tried to focus. She thought of how nice it would be to find a cute multicolored creature to reflect her moods. Better than any mood ring! Maybe when it turned bright red, and Sanny would see how much she really liked him. Then she wouldn't have to say it, wouldn't have to open herself for embarrassment, wouldn't have to be unsure of how he felt. But he really was extremely nice and attentive, like no other boy she'd ever met. Clearly, he had feelings for her. Why did it feel so good that this cute boy was so sweet to her? Could it be, she was falling for him? Could it be real? Could it be, they were falling in love?

"What do you sense?" Sanny nudged her with his elbow.

"I don't know," said Anna, taken out of her reverie. "Nothing?"

"Very good!" Sanny whispered. "I too sense nothing. This rail is empty. I am taking another one."

As he stepped off the rail, it became dark again. When a light came from underneath Sanny's skis, it was a different subway tunnel, and it seemed empty. Anna thought, they wouldn't find anything on that rail either, and she told Sanny so.

"You are learning fast. We are good together!" He glanced at her with approval, and flashed his beautiful smile.

"Maybe the next one," said Anna, just to say something. Suddenly, there was a movement in the darkness: a large, cat-sized rat scampered across the rails, except the creature was glowing with radioactive green.

"There!" screamed Anna. Sanny moved forward so fast, that the girl had to grab his belt tighter. The chase was quick – the mutant beast was cornered within seconds. From behind Sanny's shoulder, Anna saw how the young Hunter crossed his ski poles and leaned all the way forward, his face down, his long braids hanging low. The glow from the skis became brighter, surges of light running along their surface; it looked to Anna that the Hunter was channeling energy from the skis into himself, and the wyssun somehow became a part of this conduit. It seemed Sanny was focusing all of his strength, trying to lock creature in an invisible tug-of-war. Anna felt dizzy and worried she might fall, but just then the wyssun exploded in a puff of green smoke.

"So, Hannah, this is how we do it!" Sanny beamed at Anna over his shoulder. "To conquer the monster, you merge with the monster."

Anna relaxed. Hunting wyssun was not too scary after all. And Sanny definitely liked her, wanted to be with her. He said, they were good together! So what if she had to go to weird places and face weird creatures? How bad could it be?

"Once you feel the power, you know what to do. Before you know it, you will be able to take on a shapeshifter all by yourself!" Sanny laughed. Anna laughed too as they slid down the rails. It was like she imagined riding a bike with a cool boyfriend would be: her arms around him, her cheek pressed to the leather of his jacket – the kind of fantasy romance which would make all the girls in her new school die with envy. Oh, how she wished she could do something to impress this boy!

"Bring it on!" Anna whispered in Sanny's ear. She felt invincible.

The glowing in front of them became brighter, and Anna gasped: in a dead end ahead there was a wyssun. But what a wyssun! Not a pocket pet, but a six foot tall beast with a long trunk of a nose and a lone glistening eye. The creature was not moving, just sitting on its thick behind and shifting colors – purple to yellow to pink. Anna couldn't imagine how Sanny was planning to become one with something like that.

"You know what to do," said Sanny, stopping abruptly. He really expected her to fight! Her audacity vanished at once, like the little green rat in a puff of smoke. She had no idea what to do. The worst part was that, scared as she was, she didn't dare to refuse outright .

"Maybe you better do it yourself? I can't really see it from behind your back," she offered in a weak voice.

"You are right. Here you go!" said Sanny. Twisting his body, he grabbed Anna by the waist, and with one powerful movement lifted her from behind his back and repositioned her in front; he did it with such ease, like she was a lightweight backpack. As she felt his slender, yet steel-hard arm around her, Anna realized that he was immeasurably stronger than she could ever fathom, and the improbability of the situation struck her: she was skiing down the rails in a subway tunnel, in the arms of a simple-minded superhero, about to face off with a color-shifting giant rat! Anna broke down with nervous giggles.

"Pure mind, Hannah!" Sanny's whisper tickled her ear. "You are distracted!"

"I'm... sorry... it's just..." Swallowing hard to fight the hysterical laughter, Anna tried to focus her attention on the wyssun. But the huge creature looked so absurd with its single eye, its nasty trunk, and a pair of grabby little paws, that Anna kept choking on giggles, her body convulsing in Sanny's arms.

"What is happening to you?" There was real concern in his voice.

"I... can't believe... this..." She gurgled.

"You must! If you do not believe, the wyssun wins."

But Anna was already laughing. She didn't notice how the wyssun stopped shifting colors and turned neon yellow. It slowly rose on its hind legs and shuffled forward, moving out of its corner. If only Anna paid attention, she would have noticed how Sanny tensed, how his hands let go of Anna and clutched his ski poles. If only she could stop giggling, she would have realized that something was going horribly wrong. But the waves of wild laughter kept coming, until she could hardly breathe, and her eyes filled with tears. It was as if a levy broke inside Anna's soul, and all emotions she tried to control – hurt, anger, fear, jealousy – flooded her whole being, drowning her in chaos. In the meantime, the wyssuns colors grew brighter.

"It is getting stronger. This is our of order," muttered Sanny, suddenly looking confused. "Step off the skis, Hannah, stand by the wall," he ordered.

Still giggling, Anna wiped her eyes, and saw the yellow trunk coming towards her. She screamed, and jumped off Sanny's skis. Pressing her back against the cold concrete, Anna felt her heart pounding. The scene was no longer amusing.

Sanny was concentrated, staring above the creature's head. He slid towards the wyssun, slowly stretching his hand. His hand was shaking. Anna could feel enormous tension between the Hunter and the creature; it seemed, a little more, and the tension would become visible, like an electric charge. Some contest of wills was taking place: as the Hunter was puling the life out of the wyssun, the wyssun was sucking the life out of the Hunter.

What if the monster wins? thought Anna in panic, a cold knot of doubt tightening in her stomach. Oh, she wished she could strangle the hateful beast with her own hands! But, like in a nightmare, her hands wouldn't move. And, strangely enough, the stronger the hatred inside Anna's heart was, the weaker Sanny seemed to become. He looked disoriented, his back hunched, and his face froze in a pained expression.

Suddenly the wyssun flashed unbearably bright yellow, and dashed toward the Hunter; at this moment Anna heard the deafening noise of an approaching train, and then a horrible screeching of the breaks. Sanny's skis emitted a burst of light and began fading. He turned his face to Anna and said: "Zhom."

Then Sanny fell off his skis onto the tunnel floor.

The huge wyssun was swaying triumphantly above the body of the defeated Hunter, stretching its repulsive trunk stretched out towards Sanny, and blinking its monstrous eye. In the dimming light of nearly extinguished skis, Sanny's body looked so frail splayed across the subway rails. Faint sparkles coursed through his form, and began to rise like vapor, dissipating in the darkness.

The outline of Sanny's body began to shake, and Anna realized that as the light of his skis was fading, he was disappearing out of reality. The already weak light of the skis was about to go out any minute, and she would remain alone in complete darkness, face to face with the monster. The monster, strong enough to kill a Hunter. It just killed Sanny! Her dear Sanny, her first love, who was practically her boyfriend.

The foul swell of chaos which consumed Anna with wild laughter a minute ago, suddenly condensed into a dark flame somewhere in the bottom of her stomach.

"Hey, you!" she yelled, letting go of the wall. The wyssun turned its trunk to her. "Get away from him!"

She stomped her foot at the creature. The wyssun stepped back. She made another step forward. The wyssun flashed green. Anna's anger was stronger than her fear, and at that very moment all of her fury was focused on the nasty green creature.

"Merge with the monster? I'll show you a merge, I'll show you a hostile takeover!" she shouted.

The monstrous wyssun was no match to Anna's monstrous rage. She was a sea of anger, and the creature was no more than a narrow stream, flowing into the sea.

"Die already!" Anna screamed, and, to her shock, the wyssun began shaking, and then puff! exploded into a cloud of putrid dust.

She ran to Sanny's body, which at this point became solid again. Swallowing a scream, she fell on her knees by his side. Never would he shine his smile at her, never would he look at her with tenderness. It would have been good to cry right now, but her eyes were dry. The rage boiling in her heart had settled into bitter, heavy hurt. She was alone again, lost. Why did it keep happening to her? She really hated Sanny for abandoning her.

Anna cradled his suddenly heavy head. His cheeks felt cold to the touch, but his face was so sweet, even when frozen in pain. What was she thinking, of course she didn't hate him. She had been in love with him, wanted to give him her first kiss. But she never had a chance to tell him how she felt, so even if she had mustered her courage now, he couldn't hear her anymore. His lips, still curved in a grimace of suffering, were so close. The least she could do was to lean down and kiss him.

"What do you think you're doing, girl?" All of a sudden,

strong hands pulled Anna away from Sanny, and quickly patted down Sanny's body searching for something; they snatched the wyssun pouch off Sanny's belt. Before she had time to react, Anna realized, it was a middle-aged tunnel worker, wearing soiled green overalls and a hard hat with an electric torch on top.

"We've got to get this boy some help," he said matter-of-factly.

"You mean… he's not dead?" Anna couldn't believe her eyes and ears.

"He can't die."

Her love had broken the spell! She was out of the crazy Wyssun World and among real people again. And Sanny was not dead at all, he would be taken to a hospital, and get better. She would sit by his bed, and when he'd wake up, he would be so grateful she saved him, that he would immediately kiss her in front of everybody... yes, he would become her boyfriend and all the girls at her new school would be jealous... and her Mom would have to forgive her for running out, because Mom would understand. Anna's heart was singing.

The tunnel worker tucked Sanny's dim skis under his arm, and loaded his slack body on his shoulder.

"Where are you taking him?" Anna grabbed the guy's sleeve. A jingle bell tinkled, and a delicate silver bracelet sparkled on his dirty wrist. 'Just like Scout Semille's,' Anna remembered. The song in her heart died. The Scout – and it was a Scout – opened a trap door in the wall and stepped in. Desperately clutching his sleeve, Anna followed.

Chapter VI
in which Anna comes close
to losing her head

n the blink of an eye Anna was standing alone in a long well-lit corridor with smooth walls and marble floor. A light blue glow from hidden wall lamps reflected from the concave ceiling. She looked around in panic, not knowing where to run. The floor sloped slightly in one direction, so Anna ran this ramp towards a turn in the corridor. Coming around the corner she froze, astonished by what she saw; and just in time, because one more step and she would have rolled down a flight of steep stairs.

Below was a large hall, that reminded her of an underground train station, a kind of marvelous subterranean palace one can see in old postcards or exotic travel guides. A soft blue light was pouring from invisible lamps high above. Rows of tall pillars topped with elegant arches stretched by each side, framing the hall with precise geometric shadows, sweeping upward to the vaulted ceiling. The mosaics covering the walls glowed with blue and gold hues. A group of lithe figures was in motion on the reflective floor, moving and mingling without touching each other. It looked like some fantastical animated chess set. Judging by their shimmery clothes, alien-colored hair and long ears, Anna figured she was looking at the Alva Counsilors. Only two dark figures were motionless: the human Scout in his dirty overalls and Sanny's body by his feet.

She gasped and dashed down the stairs, squatting next to Sanny's body. The Counsilors stopped their motion, and turned to the girl. Their chiseled mask-like faces carried the same bored-amused expression, and their bodies swayed ever so slightly, like a field of flowers with their heads turned towards the sun.

"Scout Alen, what say you?" The voice that broke the silence made Anna's skin crawl: it sounded like a sharp blade cutting through soft silk. She looked up at the crowd but couldn't tell who spoke, it could have been any one of these beautiful and bizarre creatures. Every face now was turned to the Scout, with the same impassive attention.

"Hunter Sanny got into a zhom," reported the Scout. "I happened to be nearby and retrieved the body."

"The Danger of Disclosure?" the same precise voice inquired. There was a barely perceptible old-fashioned accent to it.

"The train couldn't move for five moments of awareness, Lord Yaret," replied the Scout.

"Five moments!" exclaimed the one addressed as Lord Yaret. "Two more moments, and the unveiling would be imminent! Was the Hunter hollow?"

"No, the Hunter was full. It's just… he at-trackted this girl." Scout Alen added reluctantly.

"This girl." There was an echo of a smile in this threatening voice, which also sounded disturbingly familiar. "So, the Hunter expired not by the wyssuns, but by the human's ill will."

"Lord Yaret, she just didn't know any better! And she beat the wyssun." Alen shot a quick glance at Anna, like he was on her side. "There was no ill will coming from her. When I came upon them, she was about to kiss him…"

"Kiss a Hunter?!" The invisible Lord Yaret seemed to gag. "What folly is this?"

She heard steps approaching, accompanied with rhythmic tinkling, then a tip of a shiny metallic boot appeared in front of her, and the other. She looked up and saw a pair of long legs belonging to a Counsilor towering above her. He turned his face down to her, staring her in the eyes. His eyes were gray, very pale and clear, but without the iridescent glow. His waist-long straight hair wasn't of any fantastic color either, just blonde. With his dark eyebrows and eyelashes, luxurious hair and striking face, he would have been quite beautiful if not for an expression of a simultaneous grin and frown, which made his face sour. His pointed ears poked through the hair a bit, but didn't look as beastly as the long elven ears of the others. It was like the alien features were diluted in him: unmistakably, he was a human, and he was a man.

His clothes, however, were completely otherworldly: underneath a carelessly half-fastened coat made from a nearly transparent material glimmered a full body armor, like a spikey scuba-diving suit, as if he'd stepped into the hall from aboard a spaceship and just threw on a robe to cover up for the sake of civility. He wore elbow-long gloves covered with an elaborate mechanical knot-work and incrusted with several crystal spheres size of a golf ball.

Looking at a man geared up like this, she fully expected to see a long sword dangling at his hip, but he didn't need to carry a weapon to look intimidating. Anna had no doubt it was Lord Yaret himself, the man whose melodic voice rang with malicious laughter, the kind of man who often smiles, but rarely with joy.

"The one precious gift you have to give away, and to waste it on a corpse!" he spoke, slightly rolling his 'r's. "Surely, I could propose a worthier candidate."

"I'll kiss whoever I want," spat out Anna, and immediately regretted it. The man stood in front of her, consuming her with his pale eyes, was scary. But Anna wasn't the kind of girl to be bullied. Fighting the weakness in her knees, she rose to her feet. He was a full head taller than her, and she jerked up her chin defiantly to face him.

"A kiss is a mighty magic," said Yaret, and licked his lips. "A first kiss even more so. A freely bestowed kiss of first love can seal or unseal a world. Dangerous little thing you are, aren't you," he continued, staring her down. "If only you could use your love as skillfully as your anger."

As much as he terrified her, suddenly, Anna felt more surprised than afraid. Not that she was proud of it, but there was truth to his words. It was like her coach would say whenever she got angry at herself for getting tired, or for messing up the technique, 'Don't waste your anger, use it.' That's what she did back in the tunnel: used her anger on the monster, and it worked. For a moment she wished Yaret pushed her a little harder – perhaps, she would muster

Desire makes reality. That's why it is dangerous not to know what you want.

Or whom.

enough anger to battle him too. It would have been nice to see him disappear in a puff of smoke!

Feeling a little more confident, Anna squared her shoulders, and asked business-like,

"So, are you the one who runs this place?"

"Nooo, I'm the one who runs errands," he drawled, his voice dripping with disdain. "What can I do for you?"

"You could send me home."

"There is nothing – almost nothing – I wouldn't want to do more to you, but see, you wouldn't leave."

"As if I haven't tried!" Anna huffed in indignation. "I would if I could."

"And why can't you, have you considered?"

"How should I know? From the very beginning, all I wanted was to go home. It's not like I want any of this..." She flailed her arms.

"Is that so?" Yaret tilted his head to one side. "Nothing binds you to this world, does it?"

She looked down. Nothing? Something did. This boy, Sanny, who now lay at her feet, breathless, who used to be so nice to her – the only boy she really loved, although she never got a chance to tell him how much...

"Just like a Hunter binds himself to a wyssun he kills, the monster binds itself to the Hunter he kills," explained Lord Yaret, nodding his head as he spoke.

"What are you talking about?"

"Well, you're the one who killed him, aren't you?"

"How dare you say that? I helped him, I beat the monster for him!"

"Alen, tell her." Yaret snapped his fingers at the Scout.

The Scout took his hard hat off and pawed through his unruly curls.

"At first, your low frequency distracted him, and you hit him from behind with the negative charge," he told Anna with an apologetic shrug.

"But he can't die! This is not for real, you're going to revive him, right? Do what you usually do, like, take time off, something or other?"

"Like, something or other," Yaret mimicked her, batting his eyelashes. "Do you think it's a trick? Do a little dance and make it better? Everything is connected. In beings, as in worlds, power flows like water in joint vessels. Every drop poured into one has to be bled from another."

Immediately, Anna thought that Yaret would probably enjoy draining the life out of her drop by drop. The way his pale eyes followed her every move was like the way a hungry cat keeps its eyes on a bird.

"In any way, never mind about him, little girl, worry about yourself," he sounded almost compassionate. "You are about to show your true colors."

He brought his gloved hands together with a startling clap, and proceeded to fold his fingers in a quick sequence of gestures. Anna's eyebrows crawled up as she saw the massive gems decorating his gloves begin to glow.

"Jealousy, fear, self-righteousness, denial, anger, anger, anger!" he muttered as the shifting colors illuminated his frowning face. "See," he said, abruptly extinguishing the laser show and putting his hands behind his back. "You are as obvious as a wyssun, and before you know it, you will be no different."

"You lie!"

He stalked around her, his armored shoulders brushing against hers. Anna felt his prickly breath on her neck as he lingered behind her back.

"I will never lie to you, that I cannot do" he sang softly into her ear. "If you ask a question true, you receive an answer true."

"I've been asking questions, and I've been receiving answers, but none of it makes any sense," she said, doing her best to ignore his uncomfortable closeness.

"Mind if I ask and you answer?" He was in front of her again, smiling.

"Whatever!"

Yaret threw his head back and ran his fingers through his blond hair. His neck was long, like a dancer's, and his jaw line impossibly sharp. "Imagine, that next to your world there is another dimension, a home to powerful monsters," he said.

"Like hell with demons?"

"I am the one asking, but yes, this is one way to look at it. Demons who can accidentally trespass into your world and corrupt everything they touch, unleashing ruin on those they're drawn to. Wouldn't you protect yourself? Set up snares and traps? It's but a simple question! Yes or no?"

"Well, yes!" By now, Anna really didn't like the direction this conversation was taking.

"And suppose, there was a way to collect some of those monsters' discarded shells – the least unsightly ones – fill them with a new, pure minds and turn them into an army of chosen warriors to hunt other demons. Wouldn't it be a grand idea?"

"Like a zombie army fighting on the side of the good guys?" Anna frowned. There was something a bit fishy about this, but then, weirder things had happened. "I guess, it makes sense," she consented, reluctantly.

"And suppose, another kind of monster with the ability to freely traverse between the planes, could be conjured and captured, and be transformed into loyal spies?"

"Look, I get it," she said rolling her eyes. "Zombie army. Elven wizards. Tamed demons. It happens in, like, every video game. So, okay, I am in a parallel world. You guys are fighting monsters, who otherwise will destroy Mankind. On behalf of Mankind, thank you very much. Now, if you could revive my friend, and I'll be on my way. How about it?"

"Funny, how Mankind always thinks it's at the center of creation, with heaven above and hell below. What if you are neither singular, nor at the center, but rather one of several? What if we are the ones under assault from creatures out of your world? What if our zombies are the lovely Hunters, like the one you are so eager to kiss; and the tamed demons being Scouts – no offence, Alen. Now do you get it?"

"So, you're saying we, humans, are like demons to this world? But this makes us evil. We are not evil! I am not evil!"

Instead of answering, Yaret snapped his fingers, and out of thin air a crystal ball appeared in his hand. He regarded it for a moment with a frown of concentration, then suddenly flipped his palm, letting the ball drop right onto the marble floor. With a loud bang the glass broke into a thousand pieces; shards flew everywhere; Anna instinctively raised her hand to her eyes.

Yaret pulled off one glove, gracefully dropped on one knee and picked up a sharp shard with his bare hand. Still on his knee, he looked up at Anna with a slight wince, stood up and held out his hand to her face. There was a tiny drop of red blood on the tip of his finger.

"If I cut myself against a shard of glass, does it make all glass evil?" Yaret lowered his voice to an intimate whisper. "No, it is only what it is."

He slowly put his finger in his mouth and sucked off the blood, staring at Anna from under the brow. Something about this gesture made the girl a little queasy, and, to her horror, not unpleasantly. Transfixed, Anna observed Yaret pull on his glove, and, like a stage magician, make some passes over the broken glass. As he swayed his hand, the pieces of glass began to move towards each other, as if magnetized; the shards gathered in a sparkling cloud, which he turned into a little twister with one quick flick of his wrist. He snapped his fingers and opened his palm. When he closed his fist again, it held a perfect crystal ball, as good as new.

"Wow!" She exhaled. "Neat trick!"

"No trick," Yaret replied. "Desire makes reality. That's why it is dangerous not to know what you want. Or whom." He looked Anna in the eyes and gave her a little wink.

No trick? Didn't he just do a trick? Anna clenched her fists. She felt a wave of rage rise from her stomach to her chest. She hated feeling helpless and confused, she hated being falsely accused, but more than anything, she simply hated this pompous Lord Yaret with his nasty suggestions and cheap magic tricks.

Oh, she really knew what she wanted, she wished the glass ball would blow up in his face!

The gloved hand holding the crystal sphere quivered, and Yaret quickly put the other hand on top of it and squeezed, making the ball re-absorb back into his glove.

"Dim and dour, my favorite kind," he muttered, narrowing his eyes at Anna. "What am I to do with you?"

"Nothing," came a quiet voice.

"Llewelys?" Yaret called without taking his eyes of Anna. "Claiming her for yourself?"

One of the Counsilors separated from the crowd, glided over and stood at Yaret's side, nearly leaning on the taller man. Anna recognized him – he was the one who recited the law to the Hunters, stopping them from killing her. Next to the fully armored Yaret he looked harmless in his fancy feathered garment, with his soft fluffy hair, iridescent eyes and delicate mouth. As much as he had shocked her before, seeing him now was almost comforting. Anna smiled at the little white wyssun on his shoulder.

"I know you well," spoke the Counsilor, cocking his head bird-like.

Now, this was presumptuous. Granted, he seemed like a nice elf, but they've only met once, and not under the best of circumstances.

"You don't know me..." started Anna.

"Quiet." Yaret raised his hand in a warning gesture. "When a Counsilor says 'I know you', it means he beholds you and your kind in all your entirety, pierces the depths of your being and thus knows all there is to know, past and present."

The Counsilor spoke carefully, as if condensing each thought to a word was causing him a great deal of effort:

"I know you. You lie to live."

Anna opened her mouth to protest again, but Yaret's gloved finger all but touched her lips. She wanted to step back, away from the Counsilors, but behind her was Sanny's motionless body, so she had nothing to do but to stand her ground.

"He means, human beings may only see what they wish to

see, free will and all," translated Yaret, making a face like he'd just smelled something foul. He didn't seem to enjoy the duties of an interpreter too much. The Counsilor smiled at him, then turned his gaze to Anna and continued:

"Our world is true, so it is unbendable. Your world is untrue, so it bends to the power of your heart. If you change your heart, you shall change your world." The Counsilor Llewelys bowed his head, indicating the end of his speech and stepped behind Yaret's back.

Suddenly, it all became clear to Anna like the glass of Lord Yaret's crystal ball. It was a test. They thought she was a loveless monster, no better than a wyssun who feeds on love, sucking it like a black hole. But they were wrong. She loved her Dad, and her Mom, and she loved her friends, even though they all – through their own fault or not – had abandoned her. So, she wasn't very good at talking about it. So, she never got to tell Dad how much she missed him, and she wasn't too nice to Mom sometimes, but it didn't mean she never felt anything...

"Okay, change of heart, I can do it" she said resolutely. "Revive Sanny so I can tell him how I feel, then I can go home. Right?"

Yaret battered his long eyelashes at her for a moment, and burst into laughter.

"It's not a game of riddle, little girl, it's a game of choice," he explained after he stopped laughing, as abruptly as he started. "See, only in human world things are tangled up together. Here they are separate. You can't have it both ways. Either he lives and you stay, or you go home and he... well, the rest wouldn't matter to you."

"But you said it yourself, if I stay I become a monster!"

"True."

"But if I leave him..."

"Aha! Now you're getting it."

She felt an ache, like he reached his cold armored hand into her chest and squeezed her heart. Faces of her friends, Mom, Dad and even James flashed before her eyes and faded into darkness.

The sadness grew inside of her, hollowing out her heart. The fairy tale turned out to be a nightmare.

What if she really died in this Wyssun Word, disappeared forever? The girls on the team would forget her by the next grade. And Mom – she would grieve of course, but with the new baby on the way, she'd get over her disappearance too. None of them cared about her that much anyway. But Sanny... Perhaps, these obnoxious aliens were right, she wasn't the most loving human being in the world, not so good at showing her feelings, but she could feel when someone loved her.

"This is becoming teeedious," drawled Yaret, "For the last time: what do you want?"

She wanted to scream, "I want to go home to the human world!" but who was she kidding. If she returned home and abandoned Sanny, it would only prove that she was the real monster.

"I don't want to be a monster," she whispered very quietly.

"What are you saying?" Yaret cocked his head with a grimace. "Speak up!"

"I want you to revive Sanny!" Anna pronounced in a firm, loud voice.

"This means you may stay here forever, which, in your case, is not long at all, because you may turn by the time this Hunter is back to his senses. He may not even recognize you."

Anna looked up at him, hoping to see mockery in his face, but Lord Yaret was serious.

She wanted to say something clever and beautiful about how wrong they all were about people in general and her in particular, that she was more than capable of true love. Instead, she simply said: "Just do it quickly, please."

"What's the sudden haste?"

"I must tell him something, before... you know."

"Oh? And what would that be?"

She simply couldn't bring herself to utter those very precious words for Yaret's long ears to hear. Lord Yaret seemed disturbed by her stubborn silence.

"I do not accept your choice." His voice trembled.

"What said is said," spoke Counsilor Llewelys. "Council concluded."

"It's a false choice!" cried Yaret. "Out of lack, not abundance!"

He was no longer playing a role. In one fluid step he crossed the distance between them, his hands twitching like he was shaking off water. At that instance Anna understood why he didn't have to carry a sword: his gloved hands were his weapon, silver light pulsating in the charged up crystals, ready to release an explosive power surge. Before Anna could recoil, he reached for her neck but grabbed her jaw instead, locking his fingers around her chin; the light blinded her and burned her skin. She clawed at his gauntlet wrist. The armor felt hot to the touch.

Her chin held in his tight grip, Yaret roughly turned her face side to side, sliding his mouth over her cheeks without touching her skin.

"Alva commands, Man yields, Wyssun pilfers," he muttered, his mouth so close that Anna could see his teeth glisten. His breath smelled like snow. "You can't command or yield. I shall spare you the indignity."

His long hair suddenly floated up, as if under water, surrounding them both. As she wondered whether he was about to strike her or kiss her, she felt her own hair raising, like from a static charge. She was caught up in his power field, unable to move, melting from inside; with horror, she realized that a moment longer, and he would possess her, just like a Hunter took over a wyssun, and the worst part was, she would welcome him. Not when the Hunters cornered her, not when she fell down the glacier, not even in the subway tunnel when fighting a monster had Anna been this scared.

"To give away love you have to have it first," he hissed through his teeth. The gloved hand lifted above his head began to glow, pulsing with electric flashes, about to strike.

"No," croaked Anna. "It's… the other way around."

The hand, squeezing her throat, faltered.

Then, through the ponding of blood in her ears, Anna heard the quiet voice of the Counsilor Llewelys: "Yaret, there is another Way."

Yaret's pale eyes widened and faint smile danced on his lips.

"Green Hills," he exhaled. "Time has no power there."

The lightning in his fist subsided. The cloud of hair, that a moment ago seemed to have a life of its own, fell down. His hand slid off her throat and caught her by the back of her neck almost tenderly. He quickly put his lips to Anna's ear and whispered:

"Brace yourself, it will be messy."

As she gasped for air, he began laughing. His wild laughter echoed in the arched ceiling. He swung his free hand with a flourish, crystals on his gloves glowed, and the space shifted. From the corner of the eye, she saw a shimmering vortex appear around her. Yaret gave her a little push, and she fell backwards tripping over Sanny's body.

Chapter VII
in which Anna sees and hears exactly what she wants

nna was lying on her back on top of her unmade bed, dressed in her ski clothes. Her room – this new room of hers – was dark, only a slanted angle of light framing the half-shut door. The space was crowded with unpacked boxes and piles of books, just like she'd left it when she left home. Home... well, Anna's new room, messy as it was, felt pretty much like the best thing in the world right now. It felt like real home.

I wonder, what happened to Sanny, thought Anna, lifting her head. *What happened? Nothing happened, because it wasn't real. It was a dream. What a strange dream!*

Stiff and groggy, she rose on her elbows, and heard two voices somewhere in the apartment: one belonged to her mother, the other to James, who must have just come home from work. Anna couldn't' make out what he was saying, but she heard her Mom's reply:

"I don't know..." Her mother's voice sounded muted, like she'd been crying.

"We'll give her some space, she'll come around," said James.

"I don't know," repeated Mom. "It's all happening so fast. Too fast for her. First her father dies, next, a new man in her mother's life, then the move to a new place..."

"It's a lot for a kid," said James. "Maybe, she could talk to a counselor. I can find out..."

"I wish she could talk to me. She hates me."

"No," James chuckled bitterly. "It's me she hates."

"James, I don't know if we should have this baby."

There was a pause, and Anna heard her heart pound in the sudden silence.

"Please, don't say that." Now it was James' turn to sound muted. "Don't say that about our future child. This is our chance to build a new life, all four of us."

"I'm afraid to lose a child I already have. I'm feel like I've already lost her."

Anna wanted to shout, it wasn't true, she wasn't lost, she was right there. She wanted to run to Mom and tell her that she didn't hate her, or the baby inside of her, or even James. She didn't hate Dad for leaving either. She wanted them to love her and she wanted to love them, it's just that she felt empty and numb.

She wished she didn't feel so alone, so disconnected. She wished she could cry.

Anna rubbed her dry eyes so hard she saw stars, except when she pulled her hands away the stars didn't disappear. She was seeing myriad of stars in the darkness, zooming at her like in a planetarium show. She was among them, and one of them, and all of them were living human hearts.

She didn't know how, but she recognized one cluster of stars, hearts connected to each other with silver strings of light. One of them was Anna's heart, connected with silver strings to her mother's heart, which in turn had glimmering threads stretching towards James' big strong heart, and more lines reaching into the mist, but still vivid; there was another little flicker of light, a thread short but bright coming right from Mom's heart to the little heart inside of her – Anna's baby brother. The moment she saw it pulsate, she felt hear own heart ache like it was about to burst. Just as the pain seemed unbearable, burst it did, exploding with silver rays, straight from Anna's heart to the unborn baby, solidifying into unbreakable strings at once. Now they were all tied with glowing silver threads, shifting and shimmering, pulsating with love, connected in one tight tangle. Everything was possible, and real and happening at once.

So what if it's a little messy, thought Anna, as the lights danced before her suddenly wet eyes. *It's beautiful.*

She felt the urge to tell everybody about the silver strings, she took in fill lungs of air… and she woke up.

She wasn't suspended in space. Neither was she in her room. As the sensations of her reality seeped in, the memories of her vision faded, until they sank deep into the most remote recesses of her mind.

Anna didn't hurry to open her eyes, not sure where she would find herself. She took a breath, and realized she was sitting on the ground, leaning with her back against something firm and warm. Her face, still damp with the tears of her dream, could feel the gentle wind carrying the scent of warm grass. She took another deep breath, and slowly lifter her eyelids. She was surrounded by grassy green hills, some with small tree groves. The hills were everywhere, horizon drowning in blue haze. A sapphire lake sparkled in the distance. And herself, she was sitting on a hilltop, back to back with someone.

Barely moving her head, she slanted her eyes and looked over her shoulder. What she saw was lots of hair, a loose wave falling down the back of the person sitting next to her. Very slowly, she inched away, feeling the slack body lean against her. The person's head softly rolled on her shoulder, and she saw Sanny.

He was alive.

What if Lord Yaret was right, and Sanny tries to kill me when he sees me? she thought in panic, lifting her hands to her eyes. They were still human hands. No longer able to contain her joy, she reached and grabbed Sanny by the shoulders.

"Sanny? It's me! Do you recognize me?"

Sanny sat straight and turned his face to her. She suppressed a gasp. The bright blue of his eyes faded ever so slightly, a faint shadow hollowed his cheeks, the outline of his lips tightened just a bit. He was an older, still a nice-looking guy, but no longer her Sanny. This new Sanny was sitting so close to Anna, yet seemed so far away.

He reached to caress Anna's cheek with the back of his hand, very gently, very differently from all the times he touched her before.

"You do not look any different," he replied slowly, his voice a little husky.

You do, thought Anna, but didn't say anything. She wanted to draw back, but was afraid to offend him. He used to make her feel so happy just by smiling, he had such a bright carefree smile. And now it was as if his light was dimmed. And yet, this new Sanny was even more dear to her than before.

"We must go." He lightly patted her on the shoulder and stood up.

"Where to?"

Without answering, Sanny started walking downhill, so there was nothing for Anna to do but get up and follow.

They came down the hill. Anna walked behind Sanny, staring at the golden locks bouncing against his back. With each step Sanny's shoulders straightened, his movements became more confident. Suddenly he stopped, sharply turned around and said, staring above Anna's head, as if to himself:

"So here I am, lived till spring. Gosh, am I tired of snow." He paused, frowning. "And all my comrades have perished."

"What?"

"The enemy artillery attack wiped out my entire platoon," he answered gravely.

Now, that was different. Had he said something about a massive wyssun attack, Anna wouldn't be surprised – after all, it would have been consistent with all the other weirdness. But an artillery attack? A platoon? Where had all the military talk come from?

"Ha-ha, very funny," she said with all the sarcasm she was capable of. "And who are we at war with, remind me, please?"

"Have you been shell-shocked? The Nazis reached as far as Moscow's walls." Sanny sounded deadly serious.

Anna stopped in her tracks.

"Are you messing with me? Nazis? What Nazis? Are you out of your mind?" she screamed, clenching her fists.

Sanny glanced at her compassionately, like she were a sick child.

"What's your name, little sister?"

"Don't pretend you don't know!" she shouted. "You know my name is Anna!"

"You don't say! You're Anya, and I'm Sanya. I mean, my name is Aleksandr," he corrected himself in a formal tone, putting a suddenly heavy hand on Anna's shoulder. "Our cause is just, and the victory will be ours. You mustn't panic, Anna. Spreading panic aids the enemy. Didn't your parents teach you anything?"

"Just shut up about my parents, okay? My father's dead, and my Mom… I probably will never see my Mom again!" Anna screamed, throwing Sanny's hand off her shoulder.

Sanny looked at her, as if trying to figure something out, then said seriously: "Forgive me, I didn't know you've lost your family. This war…"

He sighed, cast a perplexed glance around, as if trying to understand where he was.

"I hate it. And I hate to hate. Why do people hate when this world is so full of beauty? Why close their hearts to love? Why, Anna?"

"I don't know," said Anna wearily.

"Neither do I. We know so little, don't we? All I know now, I feel must keep going… I reckon… that way." And he marched forth.

Completely demoralized, Anna plopped down on the grass.

After several confident steps, Sanny's gait became hesitant, and he stopped altogether. He returned to her and said with a soft smile: "One does not tarry when in the Hills, Hunter. Let us go."

He was back to his Skier self. Anna stared at him, trying to find at least some sense in the sudden changes in his manner.

"Hey, Hannah," Sanny said a little sheepishly. "Did I say anything strange just now?"

Anna grimaced.

Why do people hate when this world is so full of beauty? Why close their hearts to love?

"Nothing stranger than usual."

"See, it is my ill memory," he continued. "When I was new, I used to remember things which are not true. They say, in the Hills the ill memory sometimes returns. You do not recall me saying anything out of order just now, do you?" he looked at her.

Anna shook her head. "I don't care," she moaned. "I just want to get out of here."

"Not I! Not yet. I feel good walking in the Hills like this. Come!"

He returned to her, reached out with his hand and pulled her up to her feet.

"Do you at least know where we're going?"

"How can I?" Sanny shrugged, carefree. "There is no snow in the Hills, no skis, so the Hills themselves are leading the way."

"So for how long are we going to wander?"

"Till the powers are in order. Till we regain the Love we lost. You know, what the Counsilors say: 'While you love, you live.'"

Anna timidly pulled Sanny's sleeve.

"So, does it mean that at this moment... you don't love at all?"

"Why," he replied without slowing down. "I love you."

Anna stopped. Looking at Sanny as he walked away, she was trying to understand herself. The words she so longed to hear brought her neither joy, nor relief. Anna's heart told her that it was not what her mind hoped for, and her heart ached.

Does it matter how he said it? All what matters is that he said he loves me, right? Anna thought. *No, what matters is that I love him.*

And she ran after him.

Anna was running, stumbling in the thick grass, when she was getting tired she would slow down to a walk. It was so quiet, she could hear the beating of her heart and the rustle of the grass under her feet. Sanny was far ahead. No matter how hard she tried, she couldn't catch up with him. Anna was sure she was running in a straight line, yet she kept having to go around some bumps and cracks in the uneven ground. Sanny's golden head was always somewhere in front of her.

It seemed, hours passed since they had stated their aimless hike. Anna looked up, and saw no sun. The sky was covered with bluish-gray clouds radiating a soft dispersed light. While Anna stopped to stare at the sky, Sanny began walking up a hill, until he all but disappeared behind the bushes of a small grove. Afraid of losing sight of him, Anna rushed on.

She ran into the grove, breathing heavily after a steep climb. Sanny was waiting. They continued side by side. Sanny kept silent, and Anna didn't know what to say. When they came out of the grove on to a hilltop, Sanny stopped and turned his gaze to the horizon. The emerald green hills turned blue in the far planes, and disappeared in a lilac haze. In all her life, Anna had never seen such deeply saturated colors. The beauty made her eyes and throat burn.

Suddenly, Sanny looked at her and said: "I am full."

He gazed off into the distance dreamily for a moment, then sat down, and began to braid his hair. When he finished, he lay back on the grass, stretching comfortably with his hands behind his head, and shut his eyes.

Exhausted, Anna sat down on the ground by Sanny's side. Looking into his serene face, she again marveled at how sweet he looked: lovely eyes, now closed; eyelashes any girl could envy; sharp cheekbones and determined chin; shapely lips capable of the brightest of smiles – now touched with a shadow of sadness hiding in the corners of his mouth. Holding her breath, Anna lay down next to him, and pressed her body against his side, with her head on his shoulder. Without opening his eyes, Sanny unbent one arm and embraced Anna. His fingers stroked her hair. Anna waited for him to kiss her. She waited for the whole of eternity.

I must tell him I love him, she said to herself. *And then we must kiss. Just like in a fairy tale, an enchanted prince in an enchanted world. The first kiss of true love is a mighty magic. It will make everything real.*

Now, now it was going to happen... Anna was lying, feeling Sanny's even breath on her forehead, and an enormous fatigue fell upon her. *Now...*, she thought, and was fast asleep.

Chapter VIII
in which Anna figures out
how the things wrap up

ursts of laughter woke her. It took her a couple of moments to realize where she was, and she noted to herself that she was getting used to preparing for the worst. This time, however, she found herself safely curled up on the floor in the corner, wrapped up in a violet fur blanket which felt like a wyssun pelt. She quickly rubbed her face: it was still her face. She was still a human girl, not a wyssun.

She peeked from under the cover. In the semi-darkness of the fireplace room she made out Sanny, and several other Hunters standing by the fire. Their quiet conversation was interrupted by laughing now and again. Anna recognized the dark-skinned Omónie leaning against the fireplace, playing with his long braids.

"...anyway, you did not lose too much time, did not wear out all that much. I almost started to think I am going to be the youngest again." Omónie elbowed Sanny in the ribs and burst into laughter.

"Yes." Sanny smiled. "I will rightfully stand beside you at the Game." Although Sanny's voice was slightly more mature, he still sounded like the old Sanny, lighthearted and cheerful.

"Better yet, let us leap over the fire together," replied Omónie.

"That would be colorful," said a Hunter unknown to Anna. "What about Hannah? Who is he with?"

Anna became all ears.

"Hannah has skis, he can get to the Game on his own," said Sanny carelessly.

"Yes, the new ones come often now." The unfamiliar Hunter shook his head, his high-tied single braid sliding like a black snake along his shoulder.

"Plenty of strong wyssuns have bread. Zhoms happen often. The more depart, the more arrive. Say, Alokee is departing soon..."

"True." A familiar voice came from the dark corner, and Anna recognized Heepi. "When Hannah arrived, I thought, he is to replace Alokee. But later I met Alokee himself at the Cape."

"What about you, what were you doing at the Cape at this season?" Omónie smirked.

"Nothing, just let my skis take me there."

"Oh, you know what they say – skis may stray, and find a bad Way!" sang Omónie, and burst into laughter. The others joined in, enjoying his joke as always. Anna scowled under her blanket – the Hunters' sense of humor was completely beyond her.

The unfamiliar Hunter shot a glance in her direction.

"Look, Hannah is up. Come on, Hannah, it is time to get ready for your first Game."

Realizing that everybody was staring at her, Anna pushed off the blanket and stood up.

"Your skis are really strange, as I have noticed," the Hunter spoke to her. His narrow black eyes in the chiseled face studied her attentively. "As if you do not love them. They are not glowing at all, and so heavy..."

"They are plastic, okay?" Anna sniped back. She was in no mood to play along.

"They are what?" The Hunter seemed surprised.

"Yuki, Hannah still has ill memory," intervened Sanny.

"How is he going to find the Way to the Game if he still has ill memory?" Yuki inquired, frowning at Anna.

Anna grew angry. It annoyed her to be reminded that the Hunters saw her as a boy. She was surprised and offended by Sanny's carelessness. Also, Sanny just made her look stupid. His clumsy attempt to defend her made it even more insulting.

"So, I'm the one with ill memory!" She said with all the

sarcasm she could muster. "Wouldn't you rather remember what you yourself were saying in the Hills?"

"Well, how can I?" answered Sanny arching his eyebrows in genuine surprise, "No one remembers what is said in the Hills."

"Please, do not tell us you do!" shouted Omónie, comically shaking his head.

Everybody laughed, and it eased the tension.

With a huff of indignation, Anna turned her back to the Hunters. Sanny shouldn't have treated her like that. Certainly not after what they'd been through together. Not after they'd been so close. Not after they almost kissed.

Suddenly Anna felt hands embracing her from behind, and a soft breath on her neck.

"Hannah!" Sanny hugged Anna affectionately, turned her around, and spoke with great seriousness: "Your first Game will be starting soon. Fill your heart with Love of All."

He was looking into her eyes, holding her in his arms, in front of everybody. He did care after all! With his golden hair back in two neat braids, he looked so handsome and grown up. Being in his arms felt like wearing the latest, coolest, most fashionable clothes, worthy of every girl's envy; it made her feel beautiful and happy. Anna immediately forgave him.

Now, she thought, *Or never.*

"Sanny, I must tell you something... something very important." So what if the others are looking at them across the room. In his arms she felt like they were alone in the whole world.

"Then say it quickly, we must get going."

"I... I love you."

"I am glad to hear it," he nodded with encouragement. "Your heart is filling with Love of All."

"No, you don't understand!" Anna panicked. Sanny didn't get it! "I love you! Only you! And you, do you love me?"

"You? Surely I do," Sanny replied hesitantly. "But you are saying it wrong, Hannah. You cannot love one thing only, and me... I cannot love only you. You either love all, or you do not love at all. You are saying strange things, Hannah."

Anna felt a bitter burn in the back of her throat, and everything became blurry. Sanny was frowning, trying to look into her face. There was neither compassion, nor affection in his clear blue eyes, only confusion. He simply didn't understand.

"But Sanny!" cried Anna, "I am here only because of you! I fell for you at first sight... you love me too, don't you? We are good together, you said it yourself!" She was sniveling, clawing at Sanny's forearms. "Don't you know how I feel?"

"I do not know how you feel," Sanny blinked at her. "And neither do you."

Instead of answering, Anna puckered up her lips and turned her face to him.

Suddenly Sanny giggled. "The face you made is just like my wyssun," he said, patting her on the cheek. "You are as funny as Omónie sometimes." He released her and stepped back to the fireplace.

Anna dropped down on the pile of wyssun skins, like she had just been sucker-punched in the stomach.

The Hunters, who a minute ago stared at Anna like curious puppies, were no longer paying attention. One after another they picked up their glowing skis, and stepped through one of the doors. After a while only Sanny and Omónie were still standing by the fireplace.

"...Yuki will be late again. His skis always choose old Ways."

"Omónie, why are you never late? You always leave last, but you always get there first."

"My skis choose better Ways."

"What do you think, do Scouts know the Place in advance, or go by a feeling, like we do? Not like they have skis to guide them."

"Ask Semille, he will be here any moment."

The door opened and closed, and Semille entered the room.

"Speak of the Scout." Omónie chuckled.

"So, Semille, tell us, how do Scouts get to the Game?" asked Sanny.

"We get on track, Hunter," replied Semille in his husky voice. "By the way, looks like it's just you and me left. Who'll be taking me on?"

The Scout was standing in the middle of the room, in full light. He looked like he just stepped in from the back streets of New York City: soiled parka, messy hair. A fresh purple bruise was visible on his cheek.

"I guess it will be Sanny. He should master his art of at-tracktion." Having said that, Omónie slid through the second door to the left of the fireplace.

In her corner, Anna grew anxious. They were forgetting about her! If Sanny was giving a lift to Semille, where did it leave her?

Sanny placed his feet on his skis and nodded to Semille, who made a step towards him, but stopped and reached into a pocket. "Wait, Hunter, I've got something for you." He pulled out a small leather pouch.

"My wyssun!" exclaimed Sanny, "I did not even notice it was missing. What happened? I never let it out of sight."

"One doesn't take a wyssun to the Hills, Hunter," said Semille meaningfully, and glared at Anna, as if she were to take his words on her account. He stepped behind Sanny's back on the tails of the Hunter's skis. The third door to the left door opened, and Sanny, with Semille in tow, disappeared behind it.

"Me, me, what about me?!" screamed Anna, rushing after them. But the door shut right in front of her. She slammed into the door, but it remained closed. "So, that's how you are?!" she cried, jumping to the next door. It was shut too. She ran from door to door, but not a single one opened.

Anna helplessly dropped to the floor. Her eyes and throat burned like she had sand thrown in her face. Everybody abandoned her. Sanny rejected her, moved on. Just like her teammates. Just like her Mom. To make things worse, she was locked in this stupid room. By now, she had tried every door in the room, and failed. She couldn't return home, and her adventure in the Wyssun World was no longer any fun. All she wanted was to catch up with Sanny, Omónie, Semille and the others, and tell them to their faces that she couldn't care less about them, especially Sanny. She slammed her fist against the floor.

"One more time, with feeling, on your head," said a husky voice.

Anna turned around. Behind her stood Semille.

"Back so soon?"

"Wipe your nose and let's go," he commanded.

"I am not interested in your stupid Game!"

"But you are, if you still want to get out of here. See, if you play it right, you can get whatever you want."

"Even go home?"

"That too. But if you prefer to stay here..." He shrugged and moved towards the door.

"Wait, I'm coming!" said Anna. She jumped up and ran to him. At this moment the fire in the fireplace exploded with amethyst sparkles and died.

"Give me your hand," said Semille. Anna stretched her hand towards the voice in the darkness. Strong fingers squeezed her palm, and Semille started walking, pulling her along. A door opened and closed. They walked in absolute darkness for some time, and she was hearing the sound of doors shutting behind them. Her feet were sinking into the soft rugs.

"Why did you come back for me?" she asked.

"You can't go to the Game by yourself, now, can you?"

"But neither can you, without a Hunter..."

"I am a Scout, I know Ways around. I went with the boys, then snuck back for you. You'll see, we'll be there before some of them."

A door slammed again. Anna heard the tapping of her ski boots on the stone floor, and realized that they must have walked into one of the ancient Homes, perhaps a cave. He was taking her deeper underground. She started to shiver.

"It's not going to hurt you, don't fret. It's just something we do every once in a while, an attunement of sorts," spoke Semille. "A rite to reaffirm the bonds of love," he added with a touch of sarcasm.

"Is it an orgy?" asked Anna in horror. She wasn't sure what that was, but knew it was nothing good.

"What? No, don't be silly. Just some innocent fun, singing, jumping over the bonfire, that kind of thing. Of course, it can get pretty carnal depending on the company, but…"

"What's carnal?"

"Never mind, kiddo. Just stay away from Lord Yaret, this much I'll tell you. Love is his weapon of choice."

"You don't have to tell me to stay away from him." Anna shuddered, remembering Yaret's prickly breath on the nape of her neck. "What a freak."

"Yes, Lord Yaret is certainly one of a kind." Semille chuckled. "Don't you know how those fairy tales go? A boy meets a strange girl in the snowy forest, or the other way around? You see, Yaret's father was an elf – I mean, Alva – and his mother was just a regular human being. Talking about carnal… anyway, it's a sad story."

"Are we… incompatible?" asked Anna, feeling queasy.

"We are awfully compatible, too much so, if you ask me. The price is high though. The only reason Yaret's mother didn't turn was because Yaret's father sacrificed himself for her. See, when they give, they give their all. His lifeforce allowed her to cross back and give birth to a child – upon which she died, of course. Now that's the stuff of legend! Anyway, little Yaret was pretty miserable among humans, being magical and with those ears. Maybe it was just poor timing: in seventh century Britain the old gods were falling out of favor, the fairy ways could get a young sorcerer in trouble. He was about done when the Alva took him Home. Don't get me wrong, they dote on him. But he never got over the hurting and the not belonging."

Anna knew a thing or two about not belonging and hurting. So, that's what made Yaret so obnoxious. For all his beauty and arrogance he did come across as a bit pathetic. Miserable all his life, surrounded by the otherworldly creatures with no human companionship for centuries... Maybe, he simply felt alone, like she felt right now.

"How could Sanny leave me like this?" She sighed.

"Well, kiddo, Omónie invited him to stand by his side at the Game. Omónie is a grand Hunter, and was the first Skier to welcome Sanny when he arrived. Sanny cannot refuse him."

Anna felt a surge of intense jealousy.

"Where does this Omónie come from, I wonder," she muttered.

"From Imperial Ethiopia. I suppose, some high altitude parts."

"Imperial Ethiopia? Where is that?"

"Not where, when. I'd say, he's from mid-eighteenth century, give or take a decade."

"How...," Anna started, but mostly out of habit: she was too tired to be surprised.

"All right," said Semille stopping unexpectedly, so that Anna bumped into him in the darkness. "I suppose whatever the outcome, you deserve to know. Here goes. There are many worlds connected by Ways. This one is a borderline world, with few inhabitants, an outpost of sorts. The Counsilors were here first. They were first in the human world too, but left long ago. There is a finite number of them now... well, plus one, you know who. He comes and goes. Three times more is the number of us, Scouts. Three times more is the number of the Hunters. The Hunters are expendable, because, strictly speaking, they are not really alive, and there is always more where they come from. A different story is us, Scouts. We can't fight monsters, but neither do we need the skis; we go back and forth and keep our memories. We are not eternal. The Counsilors – probably are, but none of us lived long enough to know. What was I saying... Ah! Hunters. What we call skis is a device which allows a Hunter to travel the Ways; there is a pair for each Hunter. A finite number, naturally. That's why when a Hunter departs, a new one arrives in his place at once, in accordance with the Four Rules. We arrive in the same way as the Hunters, but more rarely, and in accordance with the Three Rules…"

"You guys are all about rules, aren't you."

"What do you think this is, the human world? Free will is exclusive to humans. The rest of the universe is all about rules, we just play along. Anyway, the First Rule is Beauty. You've noticed how beautiful we all are, haven't you?"

Coming from an unkempt, bruised, middle-aged guy in a worn-out parka this sounded rather ridiculous, but at the same time Anna realized that Semille was talking about some other beauty. In all honesty, she had to admit that not just the Hunters, but the Counsilors, including the peculiar Yaret, and even the humble Scouts like Semille and Alen had an otherworldly quality about them, an air of persuasion, like a delicious scent or a rhythm you can't resist.

"The Second Rule is Love of All. Do you understand?"

That was what Sanny said when he broke her heart. She didn't understand him, and even now it hurt to think about it.

"Of course, I understand," she lied. "Like, being really in love with someone."

"No, no, he has to feel great love, not for one thing or person. He has to love, but not be in love, understand?"

"So, it means, none of those boys have ever been in love?"

"With the Alva, pet, it's all or nothing, so, no, during their lifetimes none of those boys had any love affairs. Whole and unspent, innocent in body and spirit, get it?"

"What's not to get," she muttered, glad that Semille couldn't see her cheeks flush in the darkness.

"The Third Rule is Yearning," continued Semille. "And you have no idea what it means. It's when the mundane just won't do. It's hard to describe. Look, you either have the yearning or you don't." His breath hitched, making him pause. Anna waited patiently.

"That's all for a Scout, and there is one more Rule for a Hunter," he said finally with some unease.

The Rule of Yearning.

No one refuses. And it's the last free choice you'll be making.

"What is it?" Anna swallowed a hard lump in her throat.

"Death on the Snow."

The walls of the cave returned a spooky echo, and Anna's heart felt heavy with sadness.

"It's got to be on the snow, otherwise we can't salvage a perfect body. See, water is the universal conductor. Snow is crystallized water, so it's a step up, in a mystical sense. Omónie was killed by a leopard while hunting alone in the Semen mountains. Yuki chose suicide over surrender when his warlord was defeated, and I guess it's been snowing that day. Heepi froze when he was caught in an avalanche on his way to a monastery in the Alps. And Sanny was gunned down when his squad of young cadets was sent to defend Moscow from the Germans in the early winter of 1941."

So, that was the war Sanny was talking about in the Hills! thought Anna. *His ill memory was no more than real memory of his life as a human boy.*

This Semille really knew everything about everybody, and was willing to teach her – in fact, he was the only one who had been really reasonable in this weird world. How foolish was she to think he was just a street bum. Perhaps, it was being an outsider that made him so special. Anna felt very ashamed of being so judgmental.

"What about you?" she asked quietly.

"I was born in Kilfenora, took a steamboat to New York in... ah, it doesn't matter." Semille gently pulled her hand. "Come on, kiddo."

"Wait," said Anna, trying to sort out her thoughts. "So, except for the Counsilors, all of you are human. All of you were tricked, abducted and kept by force, just like me."

"By force? Oh no, the Scouts are formally invited. It's a great honor, it is."

"Did you have a free choice to refuse?"

Semille gave out a short and mirthless laugh: "The Rule of Yearning, remember? No one refuses. And it's the last free choice you'll be making."

"But the monsters, the wyssun, what about them?"

"Well, pet, you are not the only living thing to cross through the veil. It's actually not that difficult under the right circumstances: passing through the fairy ring, catching the end of a rainbow, stumbling with the right foot... Critters cross all the time. Crows, dinosaurs, rats, whales – they become wyssun pretty quickly; the simpler the beast, the faster they turn. Humans take a while longer. Sometimes, it's a human on the outside, but already a raging wyssun inside – a shapeshifter, the worst kind of monster, sapping love from the world, sucking its dry until some resurrected human boy saves the day. And that's, dear girl, how the Alva keep the world running."

"Why do they even need humans? If they are such masters of the universe, can't they do without us?"

"Their whole technology – or magic, if you will – is powered by this one essential energy which they themselves cannot produce. Ironic, it is."

"And humans can," guessed Anna.

"Alva command the silver strings which bind the creation, but Mankind is the only kind of creatures that actually makes love."

A faint memory echoed in her chest with a heartache, of silver strings stitching space together, keeping stars from flying apart.

"Man yields," she said, remembering Yaret's cryptic words.

"Wyssun pilfers," continued Semille.

"And Alva commands! So, it was love Yaret was talking about. What, they can't love? But you said, when they give, they give their all..."

"Don't get me wrong, they can be wondrously affectionate. A faceted crystal enhances the flicker of a small candle manifold, yet it is not the source of light."

"But I am?"

"You have the capacity, you do," replied the Scout evasively. "Like, you're stuck on your man Sanny."

"Yeah," she said, feeling cold in the darkness. "That's why I'm stuck here."

"But that's also what has saved you, so far." He found her hand again and pulled her along. "So, no, never by force – by love."

They walked for some time. The floor was getting more and more uneven, and Anna had to grab onto Semille's arm to keep from stumbling. There was a faint glow ahead of them.

"They are gathering for the Game over there," Semille spoke again. "I can't let them see me with you. Go and look by yourself. Don't draw any attention, and don't touch the skis. I hope you know by now they're not plastic."

The glow was becoming brighter. Anna could make out the walls of the cave, as well as some stone icicles coming from the ceiling.

"Do the right thing, kiddo," whispered Semille. He let go of Anna's hand, and gently nudged her towards the light.

Chapter IX
in which Anna finds herself at the end of the rainbow

autiously, she peered from behind a stalactite. She was inside a huge cave, the size of a concert hall, its floor made of naturally faceted crystalline blocks. Gigantic pointed crystals protruded from the floor and the walls, creating a labyrinth of cross-beams. Translucent, with milky-white inclusions, mineral looked fragile, but Anna could tell the beams weighed a ton. The walls studded with smaller sharp rocks were sparkling like snow in the moonlight, more crushed crystals sprinkled on the floor. She couldn't resist picking up one pinky-sized, perfectly pointed clear crystal rod.

In the center of this spectacular cave burned a bonfire made out of skis. Upon closer look the skis were not in flames, but rather shimmering with a soft iridescent light, streaks of colors and surges of power running up and down. The peculiar game of light and shadow made Anna feel like she was inside an underwater coral reef.

The space was full. Anna saw the young Hunters in their hand-stitched leather jackets, with obligatory pouches at their belts; the ageless Counsilors in their intricate tunics; the Scouts in their street clothing. Everybody seemed happy, embracing, talking and laughing. More and more Skiers appeared from behind the crystal columns: a single Hunter, or a Hunter with a Scout behind his back. The Hunters, all like one, put their skis up to the bonfire in the middle, and each new pair of skis would lit up with the same pale iridescence.

Anna looked around in search of Semille, but the Scout was gone. She squeezed the little crystal rod in her pocket to calm her nerves.

Somewhere close music was playing which sounded like raindrops falling on tree leaves. Anna came out of hiding and went towards the music. Surrounded by a group of listeners, on a flat crystal stump sat one of the elves, pensively plucking the strings of a small harp-like instrument.

The Hunters asked for a song. The Counsilor ran his inhumanly long fingers across the strings and began playing in earnest. Anna was mesmerized. When the voice began weaving into the melody, she was sure the song was about love, although she could not make out the words. It went straight into her heart, and she immediately thought of Sanny. She had long forgiven his casual betrayal; all she wanted was to see him.

If this Game fulfills wishes, then let me find true love, she whispered to herself.

Clutching her chest, like her pounding heart was about to explode, Anna left the circle around the musician and started walking, keeping in the shadows.

She could hear bits of song and conversation, passing groups of Hunters, searching for familiar faces. It looked as if each little group of Hunters was entertained by a Counsilor. Long-eared Counsilors seemed to radiate affection, while the Hunters gathered around them with a look of adoration. The Scouts, on the contrary, kept to themselves. She could feel anticipation in the air. Something important was about to start.

Suddenly Anna heard a quiet laughter with the familiar sound of silver bells ringing in it. From behind a pillar, she spied Lord Yaret together with another elf. Yaret was leaning languidly against a crystal column, arms folded across his chest, his waist-long hair covering his narrow frame like a silk cloak, his pale face ghostly in the dim light.

The other Counsilor's caramel skin looked dark next to his scarlet hair, his huge eyes of a wild forest creature gleamed with a green hue. Just like all the others, he was fragile and bird-like, his flaming head hardly reached Yaret's chin, but there was a kind of overbearing tenderness in the way he stroked Yaret's armored shoulder.

The voices she heard were like whisper of the wind in the trees, the words were unintelligible like a distant music, and yet somehow she understood what they were saying, as if she had gained the knowledge of their alien language. Perhaps, it was the whole atmosphere of the mysterious cave, or the little crystal in her fist, but she heard their conversation clearly.

"It has been a long time since we leapt over the fire together, my dear," the red-haired elf was saying. "Perhaps, we could do it again."

"As glad as I am to see you, Féargas, I fear I make a poor companion for my heart is burdened," replied Yaret, frowning.

"If peacekeeping has grown burdensome, perhaps, for a time you could leave the outer realms and join me and my brothers in Alvaheim."

"I am not much inclined towards the comforts of Alvaheim these days."

"Yet, last time you visited you were eager to explore them." He reached up and moved a stray wisp of hair away from Yaret's furrowed brow. "We loved having you as a guest."

"I no longer wish to be a guest, my dear friend. I desire a home of my own."

"Suit yourself. As for me, I intend to enjoy this Game. I hear a human female has crossed and is yet to turn." Anna froze, realizing the conversation shifted to her. "Perhaps, I should leap over the fire with her."

"You will do no such thing." Yaret's voice suddenly rumbled like a faraway thunder. The red-haired elf answered with melodic laughter.

"She is not your mother, and you are not your father. Miracles do not repeat. Whether she chooses a dead boy, or either of us, still she loses herself."

"Nevertheless, the choice is hers."

"It always is, isn't it? But I wouldn't mind offering her a measure of amusement before she turns."

"I'll kill her with my own hands before that happens."

Nevertheless, the choice is hers.

It always is, isn't it.

His words made Anna choke, and she covered her mouth with both hands to keep quiet, but it was too late, the Counsilors had heard her.

Yaret turned his pale face to her, and the dark-skinned elf pulled away from him at once, dissolving in the darkness like a shadow.

So much for following Semille's advice, thought Anna. *Might as well face the situation head on.*

And she moved out from under the shadow of the pillar.

"You shouldn't be here," hissed Yaret, taking a step towards her.

"Desire makes reality, remember? If I am here, it means I want to be here."

"You don't say! Aren't you a quick study. With a little more time it might become possible to converse with you. Wouldn't it be lovely. Alas, you are out of time."

"You still expect me to shapeshift into a wyssun?"

"The Game reveals all. You will run out of the little that you have before it is over, and once you are hollow, you will lose yourself."

"I've gone through several Doors, skied down a glacier, fought a wyssun in the Subway, went to the Green Hills and back, and now I'm ready to play the Game, whatever it is."

"You must think you are sooo special," he drawled. "A chosen one, spirited away to a magical realm. If you only knew how many of those special-girls-turned-regular-monsters have I had to put down over the centuries."

"I am neither a chosen one, nor a monster," said Anna honestly. "I am just a regular human being."

Yaret twitched, then his face softened. It seemed to Anna that grey ice melted in his eyes, droplets sparkling on his eyelashes. For a second, she couldn't help but feel a touch of empathy for this bitter, brittle Yaret who suddenly looked like the loneliest man in the world.

"Sorry to disappoint you," she said, determined to seize the initiative. "I guess you don't get to kill the mighty shapeshifter after all. I passed the test."

"It wasn't even your test to pass," he said so smugly that all her good will towards him evaporated at once. She really felt like smacking him.

"You would have been safe in the Green Hills," he continued, as if answering his own thoughts. "Time stands still in the Hills. You should have remained there."

"Stuck there forever? Boring."

"Oh, you wouldn't have been bored, I would have seen to it."

He leaned in, so his angular face were right in front of hers; his lashes quivered as he lowered his eyelids and sucked in the air through his nose, like he was sniffing her. As she recoiled, he chuckled and stalked around her. When he spoke again his voice was like silk lace he was gathering around her, and Anna could almost feel it drape weightlessly over her shoulders.

"You can go anywhere from the Green Hills. Any place, any time, any Way. You can dream any dream you've ever dreamt, or dream up a new dream. Shine among stars? Surf the silver strings that stich through creation? Weave your own? I could have shown you."

"No, thanks!"

"Making love is a learned skill, you know."

"Gross!" cried Anna. "I want none of that. I want to go home."

"All it takes is a kiss." He materialized behind her, whispering in her ear. A flyaway strand of his hair tickled Anna's neck, and his nimble hands brushed over her arms, giving her a shiver.

"You don't give up, do you?" Anna shrugged off his hands. "There's no way I will ever want to kiss you!"

"I'm merely responding to your request." Yaret now stood in front of her, grinning. "A kiss may seal or unseal. Choose wisely."

The gloved fingers briefly caressed her chin, pulling away just before Anna swatted at him. He dodged gracefully and stepped back, laughing.

"Before I bid you farewell, one last thing: Ways change!" he added with a little wink, bowed and disappeared into the shadows.

"It is on! It is on! The Game is on!" many voices suddenly cried out. Everybody stopped the playing and the singing, and began gathering around the bonfire. There was nothing left for Anna than to join them.

The surges of light from the bonfire cast shifting reflections on the Skiers' faces. Everybody was staring into the bonfire in silence. It was so quiet that Anna could hear her own heartbeat.

She felt as if it was beating in time to another rhythm, and so were the hearts of everybody around her. The beat was growing stronger, like hundreds of drums echoing in the distance.

The Skiers began to stomp their feet to the beat; they were humming in low voices. Then a single voice started a melody over the rhythm, it sounded like one of the ethereal elves. The melody climbed higher and higher, until the voice resonated in the cavernous space, and the walls began to vibrate.

Then all went pitch black, and the singer started again:

Open your eyes to the darkness,
Path before you awaits,
Ways ring under your step.

Anna had no idea what was happening, except everything felt intense and real beyond real, as if she was delirious with a fever. The Game was on, and she still didn't know what the rules were.

Body burns out and renews.
Wings on the wind rejoice
In a flame ever bright.

As the Counsilor sang, the skis began to glow with dark ruby sparkles, like old fire awaking within the embers. The red flame was getting brighter, lighting the cave, and Anna's fear disappeared. She felt strong and alive. Her skin was tingling. She wrapped her arms around herself tightly, surprised by the sensation of her own body.

Love of All, greater than all
Quenches the night sevenfold.
Silver stars reach to each other.

The red flames of the bonfire turned ever brighter, and now glowed with an orange hue. Anna's heart was beating faster. Her emotions were getting the best of her, each as distinct and powerful as the next. She felt grateful to Semille, but also for some strange reason, to Yaret, in a different way. She felt a lot of tenderness for

Sanny, and sorry for herself just a little. It was frightening, but new and wonderful to feel so many things at once.

Nothing to know, all is known,
In starlight minds are transparent,
What will you know when you see?

The fire was getting brighter yet, until it flashed yellow. Anna realized that the color was following a familiar pattern.
After orange comes yellow, and after yellow green. This great Game was no more than some kind of spectral light show! She smirked, proud of her logic.

Deep in the mirror
Perfectly shaped vessel,
Your reflection in crystal.

Anna looked around. Now green, the light of the ski bonfire illuminated the Skiers' faces with an unreal glow. She glanced across the crowd, and saw Sanny and Omónie, with Semille behind them. Their eyes were half-shut, their bodies were swaying to the melody. They looked enchanted and enchanting, even Semille in his dirty green parka, but especially Sanny, so handsome and mature. Looking at him, Anna imagined herself an adult. It was as if she saw her grown-up face in a clear mirror, and it was everything she could ever dream of.

Celestial wind calls,
Ascends in an unending spiral
Conceiving the essence of blue.

Turquoise lightning ran up and down the bonfire of skis, gradually acquiring a blue hue. The blue followed green, just as Anna expected, but she felt that there was a greater significance to this sequence of color. The blue also corresponded to the yellow somehow, as if by turning green the color of the glow hit an invisible mark and reversed. So, just like the yellow light cleared up her thoughts, the light blue light granted her deeper insight. If she was right, she was about to find out very soon.

Mystic soul overflows,
The music of endless horizon
Turns water to ice.

The voice of the Counsilor vibrated, and the bright blue light echoed by turning deep indigo. Anna felt hopeful. It was becoming clear. Step by step, each color gave her, in turn, power of the body, feeling of the heart, and understanding of the mind.

Truly being, true to truth,
Love sufficient unto itself.
Reveal what becomes of you!

When the dark blue glow of the bonfire turned purple, Anna began to shake, new insights overwhelming her. Did she really love Sanny? Sure, it would have been nice to parade this boy in front of her Mom and the girls at her new school. And yes, it would have been nice to have a cute and caring boyfriend like that, but in all honesty, how could she take Sanny seriously? Between the things he couldn't understand about her, and the things she couldn't comprehend about him, they had nothing in common. He didn't even realize she was a girl! It was as if by looking into Sanny's eyes, she saw her own ideal reflection, sort of like by looking into Yaret's eyes, she glimpsed something she didn't want to see at all. Chasing after Sanny's love, she was no better than Yaret who kept harassing her.

Love sufficient unto itself, the song said. Maybe having Love of All meant being sufficient unto oneself. She didn't need a Sanny, or a Yaret to be her mirror. As much as she wanted her parents' and friends' understanding, in the end, she didn't need it to understand herself. Perhaps, if she wanted to find love, she could start within.

So, this was the secret of the Wyssun World's magic, this was how desire created reality. Love was not being nice to someone or desiring someone's affection, it was a force of the heart, the force that could be pointed in any direction, the energy that held creation together, and the human heart was the source where that energy was made. Being human, she had the power to make possible anything her heart desired. All she needed was to stay true.

As the singer's voice resonated in the violet air, Anna took a deep breath. Her pulse was pounding in time to the rhythm of the music. 'When the colors of the rainbow combine, they make white light,' she remembered.

Play of color, game of light,
Snow sings before falling silent,
Rainbow unites in radiant white.

The last note fell, like a single snowflake at midnight.

It seemed the Game was over, but by now Anna knew better: the Game didn't play out around the magical ski bonfire. It had been on from the moment Anna laid eyes on Sanny in the snow-covered park. She never knew the rules or the stakes, but now she knew what the prize was. Her own love was the prize, and she was the only one who could win it.

Besides, something else was happening. The fire flashed unbearably bright, white light filled the space, and Anna buried her face in her hands. When she pulled them away, it seemed her fingers were shimmering with an internal glow. She looked around. The cave was engulfed in shadow again, only a dim light coming from the now extinguished ski bonfire. But the bodies of the Skiers – Counsilors, Scouts and Hunters alike – glowed in the dark with a faint white light, just like Anna's own body.

Suddenly, a Counsilor turned to a Hunter next to him, and placed a kiss on the Hunter's lips. The Hunter in turn leaned over to a Scout by his side, and kissed him. The Scout kissed another Hunter, and he – another. As if passing kisses along a chain, the Skiers began kissing each other. There was nothing sensual about their lips touching, yet there was unmistakable affection in the way they briefly held each other's hands. Their luminous faces were solemn, as if they were participating in a religious service.

With a trembling heart Anna realized that the forest fire of kisses was converging on her.

And then, the first couple who kissed held hands and jumped over the bonfire, followed by three guys at once, two Hunters and a Scout who also held hands and leaped over the bonfire with surprising agility. The contrast of glow and shadow made it difficult to see the other side: she couldn't tell if the Skiers landed safely, and where they landed at all. But more guys were grabbing each other's hands, drawn towards the fire like moths, flying over only to disappear beyond it on the other side.

She saw Sanny making his way through the crowd towards her, Omónie was right by his side; both were beaming, not a shadow of thought in their bright eyes.

There were two more men approaching her the opposite directions. An unmistakable flaming head was floating through the crowd. She locked eyes with Féargas, and he gave her a soft grin, like one would smile at a cute puppy. For some reason, it made her sick to her stomach. Yaret was moving towards her as well, cutting through the crowd like a ski trail through fresh snow.

She turned around and saw Semille, who was looking at her intently and tapping his finger to his mouth, as if he wanted to tell her something.

Anna understood. Slowly, she held up the crystal chard and pressed it to her lips, sealing the kiss in the facets. Her lips tingled.

Without taking her eyes off the Skiers, she took one big step and then leapt over the fire. It wasn't the most graceful jump. As she landed on the other side, her right ankle reminded of itself with a dull ache, but it didn't feel bad, just real. The crystal point in her fist flashed with a faint silver light and extinguished. The ski bonfire, too, began to dim down, as if a shadow fell upon the rest of the crystal cave, forming an opaque veil between Anna and the Skiers. In a blink of an eye everything grew dark.

Sometimes, the way forward is backwards, Semille's words flashed in her memory. Trying not to panic, Anna shoved the crystal deep into her pocket and put both hands out, feeling up the space. Slowly, she walked backwards. Something toppled on her; catching it just in time, she realized that it was her skis. She took another firm step back, and bumped into an obstacle which felt flimsy, like a closet door. She pushed back, the door opened with ease, and Anna fell out backwards. Like a well-trained skier, she jumped right back on her feet at once.

She knew where she was. Her room – this new room of hers – was dark, only a slanted angle of light framing the half-shut door. The space was crowded with unpacked boxes and piles of books, just like she'd left it when she left home. Anna felt up the wall and flipped the light switch. Everything was the same, except it felt different somehow. She grinned and frowned at once, shook her head: she would try to understand it later.

She put away the skis, and removed her ski clothes; her fingers lingered for a moment inside the pocket of her ski jacket.

Somewhere inside the apartment, she heard her mother and her stepfather talking, so she followed their muted voices.

As she entered the kitchen, her mother turned to her. Mom's eyes were puffy, her makeup in serious need of retouching. James looked at her too with wary eyes, not knowing what to expect.

"Hey, guys," Anna said brightly. "I spaced out. Cleaning is a hassle, for real. So, what's for dinner?"

"Um, we could order something," replied James hesitantly.

"Sounds cool." She smiled at him. "Thanks, James."

"I've got some menus by the door." James got up so quickly he almost dropped the chair, and hurried out of the kitchen.

"So, Mom, what do you want?"

"Since when do you care?" Mom asked, only half-joking.

"Since I've got to finish setting up my room, and I was hoping we could do it together." Anna chuckled at how obvious her peace-offering came out. It was exactly the way she wanted, so she continued with a grin, "The little room, where all the boxes are right now, we could fix it up too while we're at it. We could even paint it, I don't know, some nice shade of blue."

Her mother smiled with a slightly confused expression, as if saying, "I have no idea what you're thinking."

Anna was thinking about the clear crystal in the pocket of her ski jacket. It would make a very special pendant.

Reading Group Guide

1. What did you enjoy about this book?

2. What have you read that is similar to this book?

3. What are some of the major themes of this book?

4. Who was your favorite Skier? What did you appreciate about him?

5. Do you think Hunters are dead or alive?

6. Do you think if you saw a Scout in the street you would recognize him?

7. If you could have a wyssun pet, what kind of wyssun would you get?

8. Is the winter setting of the story important to the book? In what ways?

9. Are you satisfied with the ending? Why or why not?

10. Have you ever felt anything similar to what Anna feels in the story?

11. Do you think Anna and her Mom will be getting along better after Anna survived the Wyssun World?

12. Do you think Anna's life would be better off if she remained the only child, or worse? Do you think she will be a good big sister to her baby brother?

13. Do you think James is going to be a good stepdad to Anna?

14. If you were caught into a magical Wyssun World with Sanny and Lord Yaret, would you try to stay, or keep trying to go home?

15. Do you think Llewelys was trying to help Anna or was simply doing his job? What about Alen?

16. Do you think Anna and Yaret will meet again? Would you like to read a book about it?

17. If this book was made into a movie, who would you cast as Anna? How about everybody else?

18. Take a second look at the chapter titles. Are they hints to what's going to come in the chapter? How does the color spectrum play into that?

Conversation with the Author

Print In The Snow is a fairytale that enchants children and adults alike. What is its intended audience in your own mind?

Being a devoted J.R.R. Tolkien fan, I instinctively look to his books for inspiration and guidance. *The Hobbit* was intended as a children's story, but the world and the characters developed and took on a life of their own. What grew out of the fairy tale was *The Lord Of The Rings* trilogy, and it's definitely more than a bedtime story for little kids. When I started writing *Print In The Snow*, it was a humorous, light-hearted, almost parody-like story drawing on many of my childhood interests. As I grew, the story grew as well, and more serious elements emerged. I hope that as it stands now, *Print In The Snow* has something that speaks to both young and grown-up readers, just like *The Hobbit* had for me as a kid and still has today.

In the story the theme of skiing is very prominent. Does skiing have a special significance to you?

I grew up in Russia, skiing is what you would do in winter, and the winter is nine months out of the year. I've been a skier all though my childhood, both cross-country and downhill. It's really the only sport I'm good at. When you run through the snow, you compete not against other skiers but against the elements that are so much greater than you, and that is very exciting.

In the story, Anna's first love doesn't work out the way she dreamed. Did you mean to show the fragility of first love, or is Anna's fiasco just a part of the plot?

First love is of the most formative experiences in a young person's life. But, like with most experiences, instead of just embracing it, we enter it with our own preconception. And misconceptions. So, sometimes things don't work out the way we hope. Sometimes, they work out much better. I don't think Anna's first love was a fiasco. I think this experience, like all the other life lessons that may seem painful, has made her a better person.

What is the story behind wyssuns?

The word wyssun has origins in the Russian language, having to do with the verb "to poke out" and a couple of other verbs that are not so innocent. The word is perfect for a sneaky, pokey monster; it even sounds like a little monster hissing. I started using this word in the late 80s, and for years in was an in-joke between me and my friends in Moscow. Another friend introduced it to her circle in St. Petersburg. Decades later, I've been hearing retellings of those same jokes by the kids in other towns, so the wyssuns now have a life of their own.

The book is full of amazing portraits of Anna and the creatures of the Wyssun World. Can you share more about the artist, and how these stunning illustrations came to be?

I was lucky to develop a relationship with a uniquely talented artist, Marina Botyleva. She'd just graduated from a prestigious art academy, and was rapidly gaining a cult status among her peers. She liked my story. Marina used the dolls, that I designed to embody the characters, as a starting point, and let her imagination soar. Without her gorgeous watercolors this project wouldn't have been the same.

Your first language is Russian, yet you wrote Print In The Snow in English. Did you put in any linguistic Easter Eggs that only a Russian speaker would understand?

Funny you should ask! The very early draft of this story, quite different from the final book, was written in Russian after the elaborate game between me and my dear friend Irina Maslova when were university freshmen, skiing in the Sokolniki Park in Moscow. It was filled to the brim with pop culture references, wordplay and quotes from the beloved Russian rock band *Akvarium*. Understandably, most of those in-jokes and puns didn't translate into English at all, so they didn't make it into the final story. But there are a few lines that an *Akvarium* fan might find curiously familiar.

What are your influences for this book?

I am hugely indebted to Jim Henson's *Labyrinth* as a classical heroine's journey. The story of a young person's quest through a world of monsters is as timeless as storytelling itself; each of us tells their own version. Of course, David Bowie's unforgettable Jareth the Goblin King is echoed in the character of the archetypal charismatic villain Lord Yaret.

What are your future plans for these characters?

After I finished the book, I honestly thought I was done with the characters. But then, one winter, I was down with a high fever, and had a vivid dream in which I clearly saw the story of Anna as a young adult, and what would happen if the Wyssun World caught up with her. That is how my next novel, *Over The Hills Of Green*, was born. As I was writing it, the story of Lord Yaret's origins also started coming to me, and it became the third book of *The Green Hills* trilogy.

Acknowledgments

There are many people who have directly and indirectly helped me develop and fulfill my vision, but here are those who I must thank personally:

Irina Maslova, a dear friend whose artistic imagination and athletic camaraderie helped shape the heroine's journey.

Jacob Miller, whose generous guidance and mentorship over the years allowed me to develop into the writer I am today.

Marina Botyleva, who took on my project right out of art school and used her magic to bring the characters of the Wyssun World to life with her glorious watercolors.

Everyone at Ananke Press who loved the Wyssun World so much that they took a chance on a previously published book, sharing the story with the whole new generation of readers.

Special thanks to Alex Fidelibus, the typographer extraordinaire, for his unique touch that took the cover to the next level.

My beautiful husband Nigel for putting up with my wyssun obsession and never losing his sense of humor. My parents for being ever-encouraging. All the dogs I ever loved for being the inspiration behind all the cute and silly monsters in the story.

And lastly, to the incomparable David Bowie for being my True North in every creative pursuit.

About E. V. Svetova

E. V. Svetova lives with her human mate, her canine child, and her resin dolls in New York City, next to the last natural forest on the island of Manhattan. She came up with the story about wyssuns as a kid. Over the years this tale has mutated into a monster in its own right, PRINT IN THE SNOW, which won the Gold medal in the Juvenile Fiction E-Book category of 2012 Independent Publishers Book Awards.

The Story Continues...

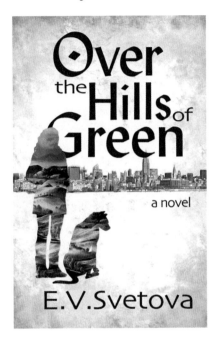

OVER THE HILLS OF GREEN is the second novel in *The Green Hills* series: A young New York psychologist takes on a patient who may be delusional or may literally come from the Otherworld of her suppressed childhood nightmares. Driven to solve the intriguing case, Anna Reilly tries to unwind the thread of John Doe's story, but instead becomes entangled in an uncertain relationship that challenges her sexuality, sanity, and her very sense of reality. When he inexplicably disappears, Anna's professional and personal life comes undone, leaving her unsure whether she is expanding her mind or losing it, and whether the androgynous John is a mystical guide or a psychopathic con artist. Finding him will either provide her with the keys to the mysteries of the universe or complete her break from reality.

Made in the USA
San Bernardino,
CA